Gun Violence  Young Adults
Death
Domestic Violence
Homecoming

Date Violence
March for Our Lives

School Stories

Prom
Junior Year
Cheerleading
Football
JROTC
Testing
Orchestra

Family
Alliance
Loyalty
Sisters
Brothers

High School 46th

Mental Health
Uncertainty
Adverse
Childhood
Experiences
Choices

Mindfulness

Yoga
Meditation
YAMHA
Self-Image

Goals
Self-Worth
Decisions

Anxiety
Depression

Friendship

Life
Interrupted

Joyce C.
Cooper

Summer Break
Vacation
Valentine's Day

Secrets
Confusion
Challenges

Self-Esteem

ALSO BY JOYCE C. COOPER


Enlightened Teaching:
Elevating Through Maslow's Hierarchy of Needs

# JOYCE C. COOPER

# High School Stories:
# Life Interrupted

Mental health is just as important as
any other health issue.

Library of Congress Number: 2018908424
ISBN: 978-0-9991177-4-3

To Angelica, AJ, and Regenia
And all students who have been impacted
By mental health and gun violence

## Ways to Connect with the High School Stories Series

Facebook ................................................@highschoolstoriesseries
Instagram.............................................@highschoolstoriesseries
Website.........www.enlightenedteaching4you.com/high-school-stories

### Website QR Code

### Snapcode

# Table of Contents

# The Summer Before Junior Year

Stockard and Stacey were strolling down International Drive in Orlando, Florida enjoying the sights and trying to decide where to eat. Stockard was happy Stacey was able to take a few vacation days to travel with her and her mother to the *Reaching the Wounded Students Conference*. Stockard was excited to join her mother on one of her work trips; however, she didn't want to spend the entire time hanging out with her. Working with her mother was okay, but she wanted to do things typical teenagers would do. Having Stacey as a companion meant that Stockard would experience the city in a new way. Trips to Orlando usually meant Disney and Universal. Her mother had promised this trip would be dedicated to exploring Orlando's other attractions.

Stacey spotted a restaurant she thought the two could agree on. Stockard checked the reviews on her phone and decided they should give it a try. Both young ladies loved pizza and pasta; Blazing Tomato had a name that was attractive, and the reviews warranted the risk from familiar chains. Just as they crossed the street to the 8100 block of International Drive, Stockard's phone rang. She knew by the ringtone it was Ashanti. Stockard figured she was on her way to work.

"I told you to ask your uncle for time off so you could come with us," Stockard greeted her friend. "I knew you would miss being here."

"Stockard," Ashanti replied, ignoring her friend's greeting, "do you remember Quin from middle school? He didn't go to Eastridge with us; he went to South Hill," Ashanti questioned and informed. Stockard could tell from her friend's voice that something was amiss. Although Ashanti could speak an entire conversation in one sentence, something about her voice was alarming and spoke of desperation.

Stockard motioned for Stacey to go to the left side of the doors to the restaurant where they stood under the "pasta" sign. Noticing that Stockard's forehead had tensed into a wrinkle, Stacey looked at her and mouthed, "What's going on?"

Stockard shrugged her shoulders and pointed to the phone. "What's going on?" she repeated her cousin's question to Ashanti.

"Quin was shot tonight!" Ashanti stated releasing a breath of astonishment and sadness.

"Shot! What happened?" Stockard questioned. She was beginning to feel her friend's sadness through the phone.

A sense of wishing she had stayed with her friend or insisted she come with them began racing through her body.

"Who?" Stacey asked as Stockard was trying to process what she had just heard.

"People are saying that a fight was going on in Cheshire Park. He tried to talk the girls out of fighting, but they wouldn't listen; more people joined in on the fight, then supposedly guns were pulled; people started running, then some guy walked up to Quin; he tried to push the guy away and run, but the gun went off and shot him in the stomach; he lost a lot of blood!" Ashanti relayed what she had heard, choking through tears she was holding back.

"Is he going to be okay?" Stockard asked, wishing even more she was with her friend. She knew Ashanti well enough to know that she was trying her best to hold it together. She couldn't resist her human nature of allowing her emotions to take over her.

"Some posts say he is on life support; other posts say he is; he is; he is; he is. I'm not sure." Ashanti tried to answer with an even greater tightness in her throat. She could not bring herself to finish her thoughts.

Stockard knew Ashanti was crying. Quin Hilton was the first guy Ashanti went out with in eighth grade. She had dated another Quin at Eastridge, which is why she made the distinction with this Quin.

"Hold on," Ashanti said. The phone was silent for less than a minute. "Stockard, that was Louisa... Quin... died... at the hospital... He lost too much blood for them to save his life..." Ashanti informed through sobs and trembles so profuse that Stockard could barely understand her words.

Stockard attempted to console her friend, "Ashanti, I'm sorry. I know he was one of your good friends." Five hundred miles was a huge distance to be able to help a friend. Stockard felt powerless. She wanted to reach through the phone and give her friend a hug, a shoulder to cry on, an ear to listen. A wireless connection was no use in a time like this.

"I used to tell him in eighth grade that he needed to stop trying to be the peacemaker in everybody's mess. There was always a bunch of drama going on in middle school. One reason why I couldn't date him was all the drama that was going on around him. One day his sister called my phone asking why I was dating her brother and what I was trying to do with him. I didn't have time for that drama, so I broke up with him," Ashanti informed her friend through an ocean of tears.

"I never knew exactly why you broke you with him. But then again, we weren't friends like that in eighth grade," Stockard replied, briefly going into deep thought and a bit of depression thinking about her middle school years.

"Yeah, that's why I broke up with him. Way too much drama for me to deal with," Ashanti continued through sniffles and sobs.

"I remember a lot of drama going on in middle school. He was always trying to be the peacemaker among a group of girls. Quin never started the drama but he seemed to get involved in it one way or the other," Stockard said. She could hear her friend was starting to cry again. "Are you okay?"

"Yeah, I'm okay; NO, I'm not okay! Quin was a good guy! He didn't deserve this! He was training hard on the football field; he was going to a couple of training camps this summer to get better. He was trying to get his strength and accuracy up to do better this season. Him and Deion had made a pact to get out of this town with football scholarships," Ashanti said giving updates on what had been going on in his life. Talking about his plans seemed to cheer her up yet she seemed frustrated.

"I wish I was there, Ashanti. I'm really sorry you have to go through all of this without me being there," Stockard said as if she was truly making a wish.

"I'll be okay until you get back. You will be back on Friday, right?" Ashanti inquired for clarity through sniffles.

"Yeah, we leave Friday morning. We should be home before 7:00," Stockard said, reassuring her friend she would be there for her.

"Will it be alright if I spend the night at your house? I could get my grandma to call your mom," Ashanti said.

"Yeah; no problem. I'll let my mom know." Stockard said before reluctantly ending the call. She turned to her cousin. "I'll tell you everything when we sit down to eat. I feel like I'm in the *Twilight Zone*."

The pair walked into the restaurant and discovered it had an open line. Stockard decided to have the spinach salad and created her own flatbread with blazing tomato, gorgonzola cheese, sundried tomatoes, chopped garlic, mushrooms, fresh basil, ham, salami, and Italian sausage topped off with a balsamic glaze and ranch on the side.

Stacey decided to play it safe and have a Caesar salad and chicken cacciatore.

Stockard recapped her conversation with Ashanti to get Stacey in the loop of what was happening in their hometown. Stacey tried to console Stockard. She knew her cousin was very sensitive about guns and violence.

Throughout dinner, Stockard reflected on their middle school years. Some of the events were familiar to Stacey because she had always been Stockard's confidant.

The food was worthy of the reviews. While they were clearing their table, Stacey suggested they continue to explore International Drive to decide what they could do the next day of their visit. She knew her cousin's attention could be diverted by the restaurants, shops, and other attractions that lined International Drive.

\*\*\*\*\*\*\*\*\*\*\*\*\*\*\*\*\*\*\*\*\*\*\*\*\*\*\*\*\*\*\*\*\*\*\*\*\*\*\*\*\*\*\*\*\*\*\*\*

Stockard was always happy to see her grandmother. She ran to her and gave a huge hug. Stockard wasn't sure why she was hugging her grandma. Was it because she was happy to be back home or because her grandma symbolized security. All she knew was that she was happy to see the woman she depended on for emotional and moral support, the matriarch and bedrock of their family.

Stockard heard her little brother in the kitchen. She could tell by his conversation that Ashanti had already arrived. She made her way to the kitchen. Her little brother was not little at all. He was taller than she and more athletic. Michael played sports year-round to fulfill his future hopes and aspirations of a professional sports career.

Michael liked having Ashanti around because it was like having another sister. He didn't argue with Ashanti like he argued with Stockard. This sometimes caused a little jealousy in Stockard. Ashanti adored Michael because her little brothers lived with her father and step-mother in another state.

"They had a vigil for Quin tonight, so my uncle gave me the night off," Ashanti told Stockard. "Can you believe that people started to fight at the vigil?" she questioned, raising her voice two octaves. "I'm glad they had police officers there. I mean like, when will they ever learn? Why can't we ever come together in peace?"

Stockard moved over to hug Ashanti. She was relieved to be home to help her friend through her grief. Ashanti didn't say it; Stockard knew her friend still had frequent contact with Quin. She learned that based on conversations they had over the past two days. She felt sorry for her friend who had experienced a lot of loss in her life. Stockard had experienced loss, too, but not in the same way Ashanti had.

"They were talking about Quin at the Y," Michael interjected himself into the conversation. "They said he went to the park to get his sister to come home."

"I heard that, too," Ashanti added.

"Some people said that they don't know whose bullet hit Quin because there were at least three guns going off at the park," Michael continued his input.

"You got a lot of information from the Y," Stockard said to her brother.

"A lot of my Y friends have brothers who go to South Hill. That's how I get all the information. Plus, some of the other guys who shoot hoops go to South Hill themselves. They said that Quin and his brothers had a plan to get out of the neighborhood. One was going to tech school and another was working in landscaping."

"People are saying a lot of things," Ashanti added. "All of these rumors about calling people out on social media and everything that has been going on - I just wish people would stop all the stuff they put on social media. I even heard that the girl called his sister out on a social media post. That's why people met at the park to fight," Ashanti rambled. It was obvious she was grieving heavily for her former boyfriend.

Michael continued to add what he heard, "Some people were saying that they kept calling each other out on Facebook, Snapchat, Kik, and Instagram. People said that Asia was getting beat. Other people said that Shaun was getting beat when the shots went off. People went to the park to see the fight. I don't think they thought it was going to be all that, though."

"People don't need to be playing around like that, either. I bet nobody thought going to the park would mean somebody would not be going back home," Stockard added.

\* \* \* \* \* \* \* \* \* \* \* \* \* \* \* \* \* \* \* \* \* \* \* \* \* \* \* \* \* \* \* \* \* \* \* \* \* \* \* \* \* \* \* \* \* \* \* \*

Chris was feeling uneasy about volunteering at FBU's Top Gun. He had only agreed to help at the camp to be around the coaches and other athletes that he might someday play with. He wasn't the snapper, punter, or kicker at his school; he was a cornerback. Quin had always been the kicker on their football teams. He was the one who played soccer every year since he was five years old. Quin had developed a kick so precise that the he was almost guaranteed a goal from the 27th yard line. Not having Quin at the camp made being there hard.

Javaris was volunteering at the camp, too. He was Quin's best friend, so Chris felt obligated to replace his tears with courage. If Javaris could volunteer, then he should, too. If Javaris and Quin's brothers could continue with life so could he. After all, his girlfriend needed him to help her get through her brother's death. He felt guilty for not being there that night. He accepted that he would have a lot of long days and sleepless nights. He would be there for whatever Shaun needed to get her through.

*****

Being cleared by his doctor two days after camp began meant everything to Chris. Instead of volunteering at the camp, he was able to join the other cornerbacks who were being coached and watched by some of the best in the nation.

Chris had torn his ACL during the state's football championship game last season. He was one of the few sophomores who had been able to move up to varsity, so he wanted to show off his skills. The coach had called a play for him to cover the tight-end; double defense had been placed on the wide-receiver, in hopes of forcing the quarterback to throw to the tight-end. It worked. Chris decided to take it a step further and sought the opportunity for an interception instead of just tackling the tight-end. He was successful in his play. SNAP! It was his knee that snapped as he was coming down from his jump into his turn. Chris instantly knew what the sound meant – out for the track season.

Chris had surgery a couple of weeks after his injury. His surgeon told him that the surgery would make his knee stronger than it was before the injury. Since Chris had a promising future, his surgeon gave his knee a few extra weeks to heal. He wanted to make sure Chris was ready for the football season. Physical therapy and working out with a trainer helped him keep up his strength and skills.

*****

Having a Football University camp in his hometown was a once in a lifetime experience for him. Volunteering for the camp was one thing, participating in the camp was completely different. Chris was determined not to make the same mistake in the future that had crippled his life since December. Although football was his game, track was the sport he used to keep in shape and increase his speed during the off-season. He never realized how much he truly enjoyed both track and football until he was sidelined this season. He was excited to get back to his life and focus on his goals.

While at the camp, Chris learned exactly how he was supposed to come out of the turn he made that torn his ACL. Even though it was a good play and the right play for him to make for his team, he needed guidance on exactly how to maneuver without getting hurt. After watching his competition, he felt that he still had what it took to get back to the status he had worked so hard to accomplish.

# Chapter 1

Eastridge High School was home to the Stallions. Everyone in the conference knew that Eastridge was almost certain to win the District's 6-A football title. After all, Eastridge had been a football powerhouse for the past four decades. Several of Eastridge's Stallions had become draft picks in the National Football League.

Football City USA, as Rock Hill was affectionately known, had produced several first, second, or third round draft picks. Burris, Clowney, Dixon, Gilmore, Hope, Joseph, Patterson, Rudolph, Sandford, Simpson, and Watson were just some of the current or former NFL players who called District 3 Stadium home for Friday night lights. Pop-warner jerseys displaying some of those same names had been retired to the local YMCA's wall of fame.

Eastridge's football opening season always began against the South Hill Mighty Lions, their hometown rival. The Mighty Lions were a football powerhouse, too. They had won the state's 4-A football championship six out of the eleven years they had been a high school. South Hill had at least one five-star and several four- and three-star players each year.

Security was heightened when the Stallions played the Mighty Lions. Two rivalries were brewing between neighborhood alliances that were zoned for Eastridge and South Hill. The fight that lead to Quin's death during the summer was a social rivalry between girls from Eastridge and South Hill. One of the rumors was that Teronience, the student from Eastridge, and Shaun were vying for the position of "Candy Girl" for a guy who had graduated South Hill two years earlier, an alliance leader with a notorious reputation. Rumor had it that the position had never been filled.

\*\*\*\*\*\*\*\*\*\*\*\*\*\*\*\*\*\*\*\*\*\*\*\*\*\*\*\*\*\*\*\*\*\*\*\*\*\*\*\*\*\*\*\*\*\*

Stockard had finally been selected to represent her homeroom on the Eastridge Homecoming Court. She had been dreaming of this day since seventh grade when her cousin's best friend, Raven, had won Miss Eastridge. Stockard spent her middle school years hoping to be as popular as Stacey but never knew how to pull it off.

When Stockard entered Eastridge High School two years ago, she was a shy freshman who suffered from anxiety and not sure of herself. Panic attacks, heart palpitations, and shaking legs were all a part of her being. She faithfully took her anxiety and depression medication every morning with her breakfast, which helped manage those symptoms. She still had a lot of personal work to do to help her get through each day.

Although she was selected to be a part of the junior varsity cheerleading squad, she felt invisible to the world. She tried out for the squad through encouragement from Stacey and Raven. They thought cheerleading would help her build her self-esteem and self-confidence. The older pair were always giving her words of encouragement and trying to boost her self-image. She never actually believed the compliments they gave her. She didn't like anything about herself except her 3C curl pattern.

Stockard had done research on the effects of chemical products on the hair and the body. She decided that relaxers were no longer the right choice for her. This led to her eighth-grade empowerment decision to go natural. Her hair had finally passed her shoulders giving her the bounce and control she was hoping for. Her natural hair made her feel liberated and allowed her to fake confidence. Going natural was like unshackling her past and rising into her future.

*****

Stockard met Ashanti in the hallway between their chemistry classes to share her news. She could not believe her own feelings about the nomination. On one hand she felt elated while on the other she wanted to crawl under a rock and hide. Although she was in her third season as a Stallion cheerleader, she was still not confident with the pseudo-attention and felt invisible to the world.

\*\*\*\*\*\*\*\*\*\*\*\*\*\*\*\*\*\*\*\*\*\*\*\*\*\*\*\*\*\*\*\*\*\*\*\*\*\*\*\*\*\*\*\*\*\*\*\*\*\*

Stockard Arianna Nicolette was truly a beauty, or at least that's what many of the football players thought. She was one of the shorter girls on campus, standing a mire 5'3". Her caramel colored skin with an olive undertone; big, almond-shaped eyes; high cheekbones; pear-shaped face; and luscious lips had many guys thinking she was out of their league. If her looks were not intimidating enough, her brains made guys think twice. Whenever teachers required students to work in groups, everyone wanted to collaborate with Stockard. She took school seriously and was all about handling her business.

Stockard had high expectations of herself and universal views about the world. The joke in the locker room was that Stockard was the type of girl you marry not someone you date in high school. At least that is what one Stallion said when the players were rating girls they wanted to date before graduating high school.

This was the talk Chris had been hearing for the past two years. He, like a dozen other guys in the junior and senior classes, were trying to get up the courage to ask her out for prom. Chris was doing more than working up the courage; he was working on some other things, too.

*************************************************

      Chris Armani Hannah was star defensive back for the Stallions. If the defensive line or linebackers were not in position to get the job done, then Chris was waiting in the back. He was usually in the corner; sometimes he played safety. He had been playing football since second grade when he played in defensive back positions for the Demons. He had grown up watching some of Eastridge, Rock Pointe, and South Hill's best players get drafted and play in the NFL. Like most teenage boys, Chris felt the way out of his hometown was through football. Although he was the best defensive back on the team, he spent his Springs running track and picked up soccer games to keep up his footwork. His mother had insisted on him playing other sports in the Spring if he was going to play football in the Fall. While in elementary school, he played soccer. Since seventh grade, he ran track.

      Chris stood 5'10", about average for the starting line-up on the football team. He had mocha colored skin, wide-slanted eyes, and high cheekbones. He had a mustache he kept trimmed and a low cut with a smooth tape-line and sea-sick waves. Every Saturday morning, Chris visited Ace at Platinum Cuts to freshened up the cut that helped give him his impeccable look. He kept his 185-pound physique in shape by eating baked meats and plenty of vegetables. He had learned a few things about healthy eating from hanging around Coach Sutton and all current and past NFL players who came back to volunteer each summer for the Demons Football Camp. Saluda Street held a wealth of knowledge for anyone who knew how to access and use it.

Chris was looking forward to homecoming. This was the first year football players would be allowed to escort nominees on the pep-rally court through a random drawing. Nominees would continue to be escorted on the football field by members of the JROTC.

**********************************************

When Stockard met Ashanti in the hall, the look on her face read, "I've been nominated for the homecoming court." Ashanti was not someone who could hide her feelings; Stockard could read her like she was reading a book.

"I got it!" Ashanti exclaimed. "I got the homecoming nomination from my homeroom!"

Stockard hugged her best friend then whispered in her ear, "I got the nomination, too."

"Are you serious?" Ashanti questioned.

"Yeah," Stockard whispered. She was still trying to resolve her feelings about the nomination.

"Are you going to accept it?" Ashanti questioned.

"I guess," Stockard shrugged her shoulders. "Do I have a choice?"

"I think you should. I know Raven and Stacey will help you," Ashanti said trying to give her friend the confidence she knew she was lacking.

Not realizing their conversation had been overheard, they turned when they heard someone speak.

"You got my vote," Javaris, one of the JROTC and track team members, said as he was passing by.

Ashanti did a 360 and asked, "Who was he talking to?"

"You, I guess." Stockard replied. Javaris had said very little to Stockard over the past two years. They had English during their freshman and sophomore years and History and Chemistry together this year. "He never says much to me in class."

"He doesn't say that much to me, either. He used to be Quin's best friend. I didn't talk to him that much in eighth grade. I was still trying to get used to being here," Ashanti informed Stockard.

"I've seen him speak to you at lunch," Stockard reminded her.

"I can't really say he's speaking to me per se or just the group," Ashanti countered.

"Either way, I'm sure it was directed at you," Stockard said.

\*\*\*\*\*\*\*\*\*\*\*\*\*\*\*\*\*\*\*\*\*\*\*\*\*\*\*\*\*\*\*\*\*\*\*\*\*\*\*\*\*\*\*\*\*\*\*\*

Ashanti Dionne Rose was another of Eastridge's junior beauties. She stood four inches taller than Stockard and three shades darker. She preferred an 18-inch, Brazilian, chestnut brown, body-wave, sew-in. She worked as a hostess two days a week at Kickstand Bar & Grill to purchase her hair, make-up, and nails. She loved the fact that people told her she had Angelia Jolie lips that she regularly colored with a lip gloss trio to get the perfect color. Working at Kickstand made her feel independent. She enjoyed helping her uncle. He provided support during the final months of her mother's life.

Ashanti's mother passed away one month into her eighth-grade school year. She and her mother had moved to the Research Triangle when she was in fourth grade. Her mother had battled gastrointestinal cancer. When her mother passed away, Ashanti's father wanted her to come live with him, her step-mother, and younger brothers. It didn't work. Her stepmother never made her feel welcomed. Ashanti felt uncomfortable with the roles she was expected to play in the home. Three months later, she returned to the Carolinas to live with her maternal grandmother and aunt.

Mrs. Bailey, Ashanti's grandmother was a retired social worker. Aunt Dionne was a home-arts teacher.

Ashanti felt welcomed with them. Her grandmother and aunt were the emotional support that saw both Ashanti and her mother through the last five years of her mother's life. Ashanti's younger cousins adored her; they thought she was the coolest person in the world.

Mrs. Bailey had chosen to live with her daughter and son-in-law to help them raise their children. She believed that children didn't need to go to after-school programs . "Children needed to spend as much time at home with family as possible," she said.

\*\*\*\*\*\*\*\*\*\*\*\*\*\*\*\*\*\*\*\*\*\*\*\*\*\*\*\*\*\*\*\*\*\*\*\*\*\*\*\*\*\*\*\*\*\*\*\*

Javaris didn't know what he was thinking when he walked down the hall a second time. He didn't know what he was thinking when he said, "You got my vote." All last year, he sat in English class with Stockard and only talked to her when he needed her help. He somewhat spoke to Ashanti during lunch when he spoke to his god-sister because they sat together.

Javaris he was eyeing Ashanti. He knew she missed his look because she was too busy talking to Stockard. He thought Ashanti was the most beautiful girl at Eastridge. He, like other guys in school, respected them and appreciated how they represented themselves. Although Ashanti was his pick for a homecoming title, he thought either one of them would signify Eastridge in a queenly fashion.

\*\*\*\*\*\*\*\*\*\*\*\*\*\*\*\*\*\*\*\*\*\*\*\*\*\*\*\*\*\*\*\*\*\*\*\*\*\*\*\*\*\*\*\*\*\*\*\*

Javaris Heyward Johns was every girl's sweet dream or beautiful nightmare. His light-brown eyes and pearly white teeth, that formed a smile to die for, were emphasized by his dark-chocolate skin. The contrast mesmerized the girls and made them do a double-take when he walked by.

He stood 6'1" and kept his hair twists neatly groomed with a tight tapeline. He didn't fit the stereotypical JROTC member; something he didn't care about. He knew becoming a member of the United States Air Force and piloting fighter jets meant the twists would have to go. In the meantime, he would sport who he was with confidence until he had to officially become a man.

Quin had been one of Javaris's homeboys since elementary school. He and Quin had agreed to join the Air Force together if Quin didn't get a football scholarship. Although he had accepted the fact Quin would not be joining him in the military, his grief over his friend had come sooner than expected.

Quin's death was something he had to deal with every day. Although they were zoned for different high schools after middle school, the pair remained best friends. Javaris's house a sanctuary for Quin. Quin often joined Javaris and his dad on father/son outings. Losing Quin was losing the brother he never had.

Javaris was big brother to two younger sisters, both of whom adored Quin like a brother, too. The void that remained when Quin passed away had yet to be filled. Javaris no longer had someone in his life he felt he could trust with this deepest secrets and desires.

# Chapter 2

Stockard was happy her mother was home when she got there. She knew exactly where to find her. The smell of garlic permeated the air as soon as she walked beyond the foyer and into the family room. With her heart palpitating, she made her way to the kitchen to tell her mother about her nomination.

"Mama!" she exclaimed, dropping her bookbag on the kitchen floor and her lunch box on the counter.

"What?" her mother asked, curious as to what had her daughter so excited.

"My homeroom nominated me for the homecoming court!" Stockard answered jumping in the air.

"Congratulations!" her mother replied with almost the same excitement.

"Ashanti got nominated by her homeroom, too!" Stockard said almost matching the enthusiasm she spoke moments earlier.

"Double excitement!" her mother exclaimed.

"Do you think I can win?"

"I KNOW you can win!" her mother exclaimed.

"Are you just saying that because you're my mother?" Stockard asked.

"I'm saying that because I'm your mama, AND I KNOW you can win," her mother said. "It's been a while since I've been in high school, so tell me how homecoming goes in 2017."

Stockard began explaining, "Each homeroom gets to nominate someone; then each class, you know Class of 2018, 2019, etc., narrows the nominations down to five by voting again."

Stockard continued, "Once each class has narrowed their nominations, the entire study body votes on the homecoming court. Only a senior girl can be voted Miss Eastridge. Everyone is voted on for Miss Stallion, Miss Crimson and Gold, and Miss Crimson and Silver."

"How is Miss Stallion chosen?"

"Basically, the ballot has all senior girls' names listed for Homecoming Queen. She carries the title of 'Miss Eastridge.' Then everyone's name is placed under a list titled Eastridge Princesses. The person with the highest number of votes gets to be Miss Stallion. First runner-up is Miss Crimson and Gold; second runner-up is Miss Crimson and Silver," Stockard described.

"That's very interesting. I like this concept instead of the titles of runner ups. Is this simply a popularity vote or is there some sort of campaigning?"

"It's both. People vote on you based on popularity. Girls hang posters and give out flyers during the campaigning process." Stockard explained.

"Okay. Let me know what you need," her mother said.

Just as Ms. Nicolette finished her comment, Stockard's phone rang. She plopped down on the barstool and placed her right elbow on the counter as she began her conversation.

"I just told her," Stockard said then paused. "You know it's okay, but I'll ask anyway." Stockard turned to her mother. "Ashanti wants to know if can come over."

"Why didn't she just come in when she dropped you off?" her mother asked.

"She had to carry her cousin to dance class since her grandma had a doctor's appointment today. You know her grandma doesn't like to do a lot of driving after she had blood tests," Stockard answered.

Without waiting for her mother's response, Stockard turned back to her phone, "She said it's okay." Stockard listened then turned to her mother, "Ashanti wants to know what you're cooking for dinner."

"I think I'll do shrimp alfredo to celebrate your nominations," her mother answered.

"She said she'll surprise you since we got nominated for the homecoming court."

"I'll call her grandmother to make sure it's okay with her," Ms. Nicolette said, assuming Ashanti would be spending the night since she was asking to come over.

"She said that's fine," Stockard informed.

"I have to go to the store to pick up a few things. I'll call her grandmother when I get in the car."

Stockard mouthed, "Okay" to her mother then turned her attention back to the phone, "What time will you be here?" She paused, "Okay, see you in about an hour."

Stockard was happy she could spend time alone. She knew her mother would be gone at least forty-five minutes, and her brother wasn't home from training. Peace!

She went upstairs and drew herself a bath. She added lavender oil to the streaming water, lit a tropical island calendar, and sat for a moment to enjoy the bliss before getting into her bath. After a few minutes, she undressed and stepped into the warm bath. She reached for her iPad-mini and pulled up her YouTube app. She selected a subliminal message entitled, "Over Anxiety, Depression, and Stress: Embrace Your Inner Self." The lights were still on, so she stepped out of the tub to switch them off. She eased back into her bath just as the ad for the video ended. *Perfect timing*, she thought.

As the music began to play, she started identifying the instruments and sounds that made the music so peaceful. She closed her eyes and placed her hands on her stomach. Singing birds joined the cello, flute, piano, and viola. She reflected on her day, giving thanks for being able to survive the excitement. She contemplated being nominated for the homecoming court. She began telling herself that she was up for the task. She knew it would require her to put herself in a place she was not necessarily comfortable being. Her cheerleading was limited to a small area on the football field; homecoming court would mean being in the center. She would have to work hard to get herself ready for the big day.

Stockard's body began to relax even more. She almost forgot she was in her bathtub as she drifted into her place of serenity. The mediation ended, drawing her back to the present moment.

She reached for her loofah sponge and bath gel. Returning the gel to its place, she thought, *This calls for a scrub.* She used the nectarine blossom and grapefruit sugar scrub. She wanted her peaceful moment to last for the remainder of her day. She squeezed the scrub onto her sponge to rub her upper body. Her legs were extended out of the water, making them easier to clean. *I can go another day without shaving,* she thought as she worked her legs. She rose from her bath and stood in the center of the tub to complete her wash. "*Ecstasy!*" she whispered to herself.

Stockard grabbed her towel just as the doorbell rang. She reached for her phone to dial Ashanti's number. Before she could complete the call, she heard voices downstairs. Her mother was home. She would keep Ashanti entertained while Stockard finished her routine.

\*\*\*\*\*\*\*\*\*\*\*\*\*\*\*\*\*\*\*\*\*\*\*\*\*\*\*\*\*\*\*\*\*\*\*\*\*\*\*\*\*\*\*\*\*\*\*\*\*\*

Ashanti ranged the doorbell just as Ms. Nicolette was pulling into the driveway. She walked to the garage to enter the house with the woman she considered her second mom. Ashanti's Aunt Dionne and grandmother treated her well, but they were still her aunt and grandmother.

Ashanti felt she had found her replacement mother in Ms. Nicolette. Her nurturing spirit and understanding ways were very similar to her own mother's ways. She was happy Stockard was still upstairs. That gave her some alone time with Ms. Nicolette.

Ashanti informed Ms. Nicolette about her nomination. She told that she won by more than fifty percent of the vote. "Only three girls in the entire homeroom were voted on," she said.

"That's great," Ms. Nicolette said. "You must be well liked by the people in your homeroom."

Ashanti could tell from the contents of the grocery bags that Ms. Nicolette was making alfredo sauce. Shrimp alfredo was a favorite dish in the Nicolette household. Seeing the ingredients made Ashanti crave Stockard's garlic bread.

"I'm excited and nervous," Ashanti added about her nomination. "I truly don't know what to do. Stockard has her cousins to help her, but I don't really have anybody to help. My cousins are younger, and I don't know how much help my aunt will be. Although she's a home-arts teacher, fashion is not her thing."

"I'm sure you'll have all the help you need. Stockard has enough cousins to share," the lady replied as both encouragement and an invitation.

Ashanti had been secretly hoping that Raven and Stacey wouldn't mind helping her, too. She loved how they gave Stockard all the support she desired. They would be there at the drop of a dime. Although they helped Ashanti whenever she was around, it was not with the same passion and enthusiasm they gave Stockard.

Ashanti flipped back into the present moment and saw Ms. Nicolette with a clove of garlic in her hand. "I smelled garlic when we walked into the house."

"I was going to bake chicken legs and make garlic mashed potatoes before Stockard came home with her news. I decided to help the two of you celebrate your nominations with one of your favorite dishes," Ms. Nicolette explained.

"I never saw anyone make fresh alfredo sauce. You always have it made when I get here."

Ashanti missed being able to cook with her mother. She worked at Kickstand as a hostess. That was what her uncles would allow her to do. What she really wanted to do was work in the kitchen.

Ever since she was in fifth grade, she secretly wanted to become a chef and own her own restaurant. Her mother began teaching her to cook when they first moved to the Triangle. She never got all the lessons she wanted from her mother due to her mother's reaction to the chemotherapy and radiation.

She watched Ms. Nicolette pluck another clove from the bulb of garlic. "Do you need help with anything?" Ashanti inquired.

"I could use some help," Ms. Nicolette answered. Although she could handle the kitchen on her own, something about the request said the child needed something more than dinner.

"What would you like me to do?" Ashanti asked.

"What would you like to learn?" the mother inquired.

"How to make alfredo sauce from scratch," Ashanti answered as delight leaped into her heart.

"I think I'll just take you through the entire meal. We'll save the garlic bread for your friend. I suspect she will be here just before it's time to get the bread ready for the oven."

Ashanti admired how Ms. Nicolette knew Stockard so well. The mother peeled a few more cloves from the bulb then laid them to the side. She showed Ashanti how to peel shrimp.

"I don't like my shrimp pre-cook or pre-peeled. I prefer my shrimp to be wild caught. They have a different taste all together," Ms. Nicolette informed.

Ashanti looked at her mother-figure intently. She began to understand why her friend had such a sophisticated palate. Stockard carried her lunch to school because she didn't like school lunch. She thought it was too bland and lacked nutrition.

"One day," Ms. Nicolette began to tell Ashanti a story, "when we were at the beach, we decided to drive north on the coast to get our supply of shrimp. Shrimp fresh off the boat is truly wild caught. We walked to the dock to survey the best deal. The guy we bought our shrimp from had a sign that read, 'Friends don't let friends buy imported shrimp.' I thought that was hilarious," the mother said giving a slight laugh.

"That was funny," Ashanti said. She wasn't sure if she was referring to the sign or Ms. Nicolette's laugh.

Next, Ms. Nicolette showed Ashanti how to use a garlic press. She explained how unsalted butter would keep the garlic and butter from burning. Ashanti placed a stick of butter in the caste iron skillet and melted it on low heat. Then she added garlic by using the pressing technique she was just shown.

"Did you save enough cloves for me?" Stockard asked as she entered the kitchen.

"I think so," her mother answered.

Ashanti was instructed to add heavy whipping cream and grated parmesan cheese to the skillet. This was the first time she used a grate for parmesan cheese. Her family usually brought grated cheese. Ms. Nicolette explained that cheese loses some of it flavor when it has been pre-shredded or grated.

"Cheese loses some of its sharpness when cellulose is added," she explained. "That's why I purchase cheese in blocks and shred it myself."

"Mama, it sounds like the pasta might be done," Stockard said raising her mother's attention to the other burner. She knew her mom was focused on teaching Ashanti, so she reminded her of the other thing going on in the kitchen.

After Ms. Nicolette took care of the pasta, she returned to the sauce Ashanti was making. She told Stockard she could begin work on the bread as she pulled out another caste iron skillet.

Ashanti watched Stockard soften salted butter in the microwave. She added a drizzle of olive oil, crushed red peppers, Italian seasoning, and pressed garlic to the butter. She spread the mixture on slices of Italian bread.

Stockard sat the table while the bread heated. Michael came home just in time to join them. Stockard was happy she had included him in the count.

"I've been thinking about going to culinary school," Ashanti stated, not realizing she had confessed one of her deepest secrets.

"Culinary school is a good choice," Ms. Nicolette said trying to give the encouragement she thought Ashanti's own mother would to give.

"I'm not so sure how my grandma and aunt would feel about that. They want me to be a nurse, teacher, or social workers. I'm not feeling it," Ashanti said. "I like being in a kitchen and working with fresh ingredients," she confessed.

"I'm sure they will support your dreams," the mother said. "Your grandmother and aunt want you to be happy."

"I hope so," Ashanti said. "They don't cook the way you do and my mama did." She had learned about nutrition and wholistic health when her mother was battling cancer. One reason she desired to become a chef was to offer nutrition foods that would prevent people from getting cancer, diabetes, and high blood pressure. Ashanti was so deep in thought that she barely heard what Stockard was saying.

"Stacey called while I was upstairs. I told her about our nominations. She said that she and Raven would help us if we needed them to. I already accepted the offer, Ashanti."

Ashanti felt relieved. Her wish had come true.

*****************************************************

Things in the locker room were beginning to heat up for Chris. Rumors were spreading about Shaun vying to be some dude's "Candy Girl." He didn't believe all the things people were saying. Shaun had been his girl for almost a year. She was the one who chased him until he finally gave in. He trusted her! There was no way she would betray him.

After a couple days of hearing the rumors, his urge to find out the truth got the best of him. Morning conditioning was bringing more heat than he needed to get through his school day.

He saw Asia coming from her gym class and decided to get her version of what lead up to that day in the park. "Asia, can I talk to you for a minute?" Chris asked.

She was hesitant but stopped any way. "What's up?" she asked.

"Is everything cool between you and Shaun?" Chris asked.

"Why don't you ask her," she responded.

"I have but I'm asking you now. What's up?" Chris asked again.

"Everything's cool with me," Asia answered.

"Look, what was the fight in the park about?" Chris asked.

"Chris, I really don't want to talk about all that. I wish it never happened," Asia clarified.

"Me, too. But it did. What was the fight about? Quin was one of my boys!" Chris said.

"What do you think it was about?" she asked.

"Girl drama. People talking too much. People boosting up a fight," sharing his thoughts with Asia.

"Then you got it," she said as she walked away.

Chris had made no more progress than he had before he stopped her. He wanted to ask her if the "Candy Girl" stuff was true, but he wasn't sure he was ready for the answer to be, "Yes."

The warning bell rang for the next class. Chris sprinted to his class. The rumors, the conversation, and Quin's death were beginning to make him feel "crazy." None of this stuff made any sense. At times, he knew that his girlfriend could be a little messy and have drama going on over nothing. She was having a hard time getting used to life without her brother. He had taken so many "punches" from her since June. When she was in one of her terrible moods, he did everything he could to help get her through the moment. He was grieving, just like so many other people, over Quin's death. Regardless of how he was feeling, nothing could match how Shaun must be feeling.

Chris tried his best to focus throughout the day. He reminded himself of his goals, but that didn't help him much. He continued to think about Shaun. He wanted her to put the same amount of effort in their relationship that she had in the beginning.

Things had changed between them, even before Quin's death. He could not blame in on grief. Everything people were saying was getting to him.

# Chapter 3

Stockard was feeling anxious coming up to the Monday morning after the second vote. Uneasiness flooded her mind about getting and not getting the second-round vote. She panicked just thinking about moving out from the spot on the football field that had become her home since freshman year. Once a space had become hers, she didn't want to leave it. Another thought crossed her mind. Could she deal with the rejection of not being selected to represent the junior class on the homecoming court?

Walking outside from building to building to get to her classes had been a big deal for her. She worked with her therapist every week for the first semester of her freshman year to get adjusted to the change. Her psychiatrist increased her anxiety medication and visits to her office while her body adjusted to the increase.

Stockard first began having suicidal thoughts in fifth grade. Those thoughts intensified while in middle school. Cheerleading and orchestra gave her reasons to fight through her hopelessness and her desires to stay home. She knew her squad mates needed her, which is why she pushed herself to get up when she didn't want to. A fleeting thought entered her mind.

For a moment Stockard felt like she might go into an abyss. She whispered her mantra, "I AM important to myself and people around me. I have a purpose in life. I AM cherished!"

ENN, Eastridge News Network, came on for the morning updates. The weather forecast came first. The sizzle reel highlighting the Stallion's game against the Rock Pointe Trojans flashed across the screen next. Results from the Bearcat and Mighty Lions game closed the sport segment. Important news juniors and seniors needed to be aware of - info about colleges and universities that would be visiting for the week and companies soliciting employees - created even greater tension in Stockard.

Finally, a list of nominees who were chosen to be a member of the homecoming court was announced. Freshman names were given first. When it got to the junior class, Stockard was surprised to hear both her name and Ashanti's name announced. She was so overjoyed, that she broke the school rule about cell phones and texted her mother and cousins.

\*\*\*\*\*\*\*\*\*\*\*\*\*\*\*\*\*\*\*\*\*\*\*\*\*\*\*\*\*\*\*\*\*\*\*\*\*\*\*\*\*\*\*\*\*\*\*\*\*\*

Stockard decided to sit with Ashanti and her friends from gym class during lunch. Javaris and Chris walked up and joined them. Brenna, Javaris's god-sister turned to him and asked, "What do y'all want?"

Javaris didn't like Brenna's attitude. "We just came over to congratulate Ashanti and Stockard for being on the homecoming court," he answered.

"And," Brenna added.

"Don't be mad because nobody voted for you," Javaris added. "If you get rid of that attitude, maybe you will get the vote next time."

"Whatever," Brenna replied flickering her braids over her shoulder, while turning to face the group at the adjacent table.

"So, who's escorting you at the pep-rally?" Chris whispered to Stockard.

"I don't know," Stockard answered.

"I can do it if you want me to," Chris whispered again.

"Is that in the rules?" Stockard asked. "I thought pep-rally escorts were randomly selected."

"I can pull some strings," Chris said.

"Don't you have a girlfriend?" Stockard asked.

"Not anymore," Chris answered.

"Oh, okay," Stockard said. "What happened?" she asked.

"He probably hit her! You know he has a bad temper, especially when he is taking them 'roids." Brenna said turning from the other group.

Chris slapped the air beside him with his left hand. "Forget you," he said directing his comment to Brenna as he stood up.

"You don't care what you say," Javaris addressed his god-sister. "Stop talking so much."

"Am I lying? Huh? Am I lying?" Brenna inquired.

"You don't know what you're talking about," Javaris said.

"What happened then, Chris. Huh, huh?" Brenna asked leaning over to Chris while craning her head in Chris's direction.

"It's none of your business. We just broke up," he answered.

"Did you cheat on her, too?" Brenna asked.

"Let's go, Chris," Javaris said. "It's time to go." Javaris led his friend in the direction of the breezeway.

"What was that all about?" Ashanti asked Brenna.

"Chris gets on my nerves with his cocky self," Brenna answered. "That's all."

"It sounded like it was more than that," Ashanti replied.

"Chris dated Shayla last year," said Rian, one of the girls from gym class. She started telling the history about the drama.

"Shayla told everybody that Chris hit her and cheated on her. She showed Brenna a bruise she got when he pushed her into a wall. You know Shayla and Brenna are best friends, so she's still a little sour over what Chris did to Shayla. I think Brenna and Quin dated when Shaun and Chris dated. Shaun told Brenna that Chris hit her and cheated on her, too. Brenna and Quin were still friends when he died. People still dealing with all that stuff. You see she still has his obituary in her binder."

"You used to date Quin?" Ashanti asked Brenna.

"It was more of a downlow, off-and-on dating," Rian continued. "Quin had been hitting that since eighth grade. I don't think they ever completely stopped. You know how that goes."

"Are you serious?" Ashanti asked.

"Quin used to hit that on a regular when he went to his daddy's house," Rian said.

"Are you serious?" Ashanti asked again.

"What's up with you?" Rian asked. "You act like you were in love with Quin or something."

"Quin was a friend of mine," Ashanti answered.

Rian read the look on Ashanti's face, "Oh, I didn't know. I forgot, you didn't go to the Creek with us. I guess you never heard."

"No, I didn't," Ashanti answered. "I went to the Road with Quin."

Ashanti was happy lunch was over. The bell gave her the out she was looking for to leave the group. Stockard walked towards the breezeway with Ashanti. She wanted to be a source of comfort before they parted.

"I will meet you in the parking lot," Stockard said to her friend. She realized the blow was one more thing Ashanti had to deal with.

**************************************************

"Quin would never answer his phone when he was at his daddy's house," Ashanti said to Stockard. "He said that his daddy had him doing a lot of chores and stuff. I can't believe I thought about having sex with him, too," Ashanti said with tears forming in her eyes. "He pressured me so much that I almost gave in.

Breaking up with him was the best thing. I can see that now. My grandma would've KILLED me if I had done something like that," she said. Tears were making their way down her cheeks.

Stockard didn't know what to say. She could only imagine the betrayal Ashanti felt. She knew Ashanti and Quin were a couple in middle school but never imagined how deep the relationship went.

Stockard remembered Ashanti sharing how Quin was a big help when she was adjusting to being in Rock Hill after she moved in eighth grade. Stockard had learned quite a bit about their relationship during the summer.

"I got in trouble with him by Mrs. Horton when she caught us kissing in the computer lab. She didn't call my grandma but gave me lunch detention for an entire week!" Ashanti exclaimed.

"Another time when we were outside, I went behind the concession stand. I was so messed up that I thought he really loved me. Just to think; I almost sneaked out of my grandma's house a couple of times to be with him," Ashanti spoke with a tightness in her throat.

Ashanti was crying over Quin's unfaithfulness. Stockard felt sympathy for her friend but didn't have the right words to say. Romantic relationships were not Stockard's area of expertise.

Finally, Stockard asked, "What happened when you went behind the concessions stand?"

"I let him kiss me again. He tried to put his hands in other places, so I ran back to the basketball courts."

Ashanti lifted her head and looked through the windshield; she spotted Javaris walking to his car. She switched on the engine, powered down the driver's side window, and called to him to come to her. She motioned for him to take the back seat as he approached the vehicle; he complied.

Immediately, Javaris could tell Ashanti had been crying. Quin had told him how much she cried when she moved here. Feeling sympathy for her, he wondered why she was crying now. He didn't know what he could do to comfort the girl that had experienced so many disappoints in her life.

"Did you know about Quin and Brenna?" Ashanti turned in her seat to face him just as he was entering the car.

"Know what?" Javaris asked shrugging his shoulders.

"Rian told her everything," Stockard offered trying to save her friend the agony of doing so.

"If you're talking about Quin and Brenna, you know how boys are," Javaris offered as an explanation.

"No, I don't!" Ashanti said fiercely.

"Look," Javaris began, "be happy you didn't do the things other girls did. Quin really respected you for that. He cared about you, girl."

"Is that supposed to make me feel better?"

"He said that out of all the girls he dated, you were the one he liked the most," Javaris further explained.

"Is that supposed to make me feel better, too?" Ashanti questioned.

"I don't know what to say. Quin was my friend, and friends keep secrets. He was used to things you didn't do. He wasn't used to having that type of relationship. He tried to make it work," Javaris continued.

"I thought he cared about me," Ashanti whispered to herself.

"He did," Javaris said. "He was hurt when you broke up with him. Trust me on this!"

"It sure doesn't feel that way," Ashanti whispered again.

Javaris and Stockard dropped their heads. Neither of them knew what to say. The three of them sat in silence for a few minutes.

Javaris broke the silence when he smiled and said, "Congratulations on winning the nomination for the homecoming court. I can escort one of you on the field if you want me to. I just have to let my colonel know which one."

Stockard turned her gaze from her friend to Javaris. "That's so nice of you, Javaris." Sensing her friend's pain, she said to Javaris, "You can escort Ashanti."

"Okay, I'll do that if that's okay with you," Javaris address Ashanti.

Still in her daze, Ashanti answered, "I guess."

Ashanti and Stockard's phones seemed to vibrate simultaneously. They had been in the parking lot for almost an hour since school ended. Stockard usually called her mother to let her know she wasn't coming home immediately after school. Ashanti's grandmother required her check-in, too. The girls assumed it was their caregivers who were ringing their phones to find out where they were.

"I guess I better go," Javaris said, dropping his head as they answered their phones. He opened the back door and slid out. He sauntered to his car.

"I'm sorry," Stockard said. "We are on our way home now." She looked over at her friend. "Ashanti wants to know if she can spend the night at our house."

Ashanti looked up at her friend; she was amazed at how in-tuned Stockard was to her. That was one of the main reasons they were best friends. Stockard seemed to know what she needed, sometimes even before she did.

"Okay, we'll go to her house first before I come home," Stockard informed her mother.

**********************************************

When Stockard and Ashanti walked into the kitchen, Ms. Nicolette knew she was needed to be a source of comfort. Ashanti's eyes were swollen and red, indicating she had been crying. Ms. Nicolette assumed she was needed to be an ear or give words of encouragement.

"I decided to make hamburgers and homemade fries tonight," Ms. Nicolette informed the girls.

"Thanks," the girls said in unison. Food was the last thing on their minds.

"So, tell me about the homecoming results," Ms. Nicolette requested. She wanted to talk about something that would ease whatever was going on.

"We both made it," Stockard answered without the expected enthusiasm that comes with the accomplishment.

"That's exciting," Ms. Nicolette answered with a glow on her face. "What else happened at school today?"

Stockard looked at her friend then asked, "Can I tell her?"

"I don't care," Ashanti answered. In that moment Ashanti felt that she could use a mother's advice. HER mother's advice. She listened as Stockard told her mother what happened during lunch and after school, sparing no details.

Ms. Nicolette had always told Stockard to call her if she was in trouble and to do so as soon as the trouble started. This didn't qualify as trouble; nevertheless, it was a moment of substantial need.

"I'm going to take a shower before we eat," Stockard said leaving Ashanti to be alone with her mother. She was selfless with her mother when it came to Ashanti because she knew her friend needed a mother. Grandmothers were cool and all, but mothers were just that, mothers.

"How do you feel about all of this?" Ms. Nicolette asked Ashanti as she moved closer to her to rub her right shoulder and look more directly in her face.

Ashanti turned and immediately wrapped her arms around her neck. "I NEED MY MAMA!" she wept.

Ms. Nicolette wrapped her arms around the child who seemed to be carrying the world on her shoulders. She could only imagine what this child was going through. She wanted to offer words of wisdom but decided to remain silent. The last thing the young lady needed was advice. She needed an embrace and a source of comfort.

\*\*\*\*\*\*\*\*\*\*\*\*\*\*\*\*\*\*\*\*\*\*\*\*\*\*\*\*\*\*\*\*\*\*\*\*\*\*\*\*\*\*\*\*\*\*\*\*\*\*

Javaris called his friend when he thought he was home from football practice. "What's up?" he asked.

"Nothing much; just gettin' in from practice," he replied. Chris was pushing himself to block out distractions and focus on his plans. He wanted to maintain his status on the football field, which was why he had to let the relationship with Shaun go. He didn't need to get caught up in some of the drama that added insult to his injury last year.

"Man, Brenna talks too much. You know she kept going on after you left. Ashanti didn't know that Quin used to talk to ole' girl," Javaris informed.

"Ashanti is one of those girls you don't go too far with. Quin had to do something. You know how he was. Is that what she was mad about?" Chris asked.

"Man, I don't know. She still trippin' over Shayla. By the way, when did you and Shaun break up?" Javaris inquired.

"A couple of days ago," Chris answered.

"Think y'all gonna get back together?"

"Man, I'm through wit' all that. I just wanna' focus on getting my work done and football for right now," Chris answered. Secretly he wanted to cry. Stallions don't give in to that kind of weakness.

"Was it the mouth?" Javaris inquired.

"Other things, too. Girls are always running up to me and stuff. Next time, I'm dating a girl that doesn't run after me. I'm going to attract her," Chris said.

"How you gonna' make that happen with girls throwing themselves all over you?" Javaris asked.

"Hit it and quit it. It's time out for serious relationships, man," Chris answered.

He was rubbing his left hand over his short hair. He was still in disbelief over what he had seen two nights before. There was nothing Shaun could say to him that would make him go back.

"People be playin' too many games, man. I just don't get girls acting worse than dudes," Chris said, reflecting on the night he ended his relationship with Shaun and the day he ended things with Shayla.

"What you mean by that?" Javaris grilled.

"Just what I said. Girls acting worse than dudes." Chris switched the phone to his left hand. He massaged his left shoulder with his right hand.

Chris told his trainer the injuries to his shoulder came from tripping over his dog and hitting the concrete columns on his front porch. In truth he had taken yet another punch from Shaun.

When Chris saw Shaun getting out of Hawk's car, he knew the "Candy Girl" stories had to be true. When Hawk drove off, he confronted her. The exchange led to Shaun pushing him so he left. She later came to his house to confront him. Things go heated. He walked her to his front porch and told her to leave. She started punching and kicking him. He grabbed her by the arms and pushed her from him.

That's when Monique, the girl who drove Shaun to Chris's house, got out of her car and joined in on the attack. He stumbled into the columns on his front porch. Then they left.

Chris was a bit dazed and confused. He decided that was the last time he was going to accept abuse from a girl. That night would the be last time he dated someone who asked him out. The next girl he dated would be someone he pursued. He was going to college and wanted a girl with the same goals. It was time out for the drama.

"Did you hit Shayla?" Javaris interrogated, intruding on Chris's memories.

"What kinda crazy question is that? I don't hit girls!" Chris insisted, feeling insulted.

If Javaris and the guys in the locker room knew the punches he had taken from girls, would they still respect him the same? Whether he was the abuser or the abused, both carried a weight that made people look at him suspiciously. Chris dropped his head feeling a sense of defeat.

"Why Brenna keep saying that?" Javaris asked.

"I don't know, and I don't care! I know at times I have a temper during football season. That's because I'm focused on what I need to do and don't like people getting in my face and distracting me when I need to concentrate. Game day is even worse. I don't hit girls, and I wish she would stop saying stuff like that!" Chris said feeling frustrated. There was no way he could protect himself by telling the truth.

"Getting a little piece on the side because girls be throwing it at you like they're throwing a frisbee does not count as cheating," Javaris said while in deep thought. He could sense Chris's frustrations with the accusations and rumors.

"Especially if they not gonna be your girlfriend," Chris said.

"Yep, especially if they not gonna be your girlfriend," Javaris said. Needing to end the conversation and get ready for tomorrow, Javaris said, "Hey, man. I've got to go. I need to work on a History assignment."

"Catch you tomorrow," Chris repeated.

# Chapter 4

Ashanti was beginning to feel like the sister Stockard never had. She was spending at least two nights a week at her house. Her grandmother and aunt agreed. They trusted the Nicolette home and felt it would be good for Ashanti's mental health. Stacey and Raven had come to help them get ready for homecoming.

During their Fall break, the older duo had taken the younger duo shopping for the outfits they would wear to the pep-rally and the dresses they would wear on the field. They had returned the night before to get them ready. Raven was gearing up to use her expertise to help the girls win. The art of beauty was here specialty.

Stockard had chosen to wear high-rise skinny jeans, tulip-hemmed in Hayes wash. She selected a soft-blue, stitch-mix mocked sweater tank. She wore black ankle-length boots with a silver chain around the heel. Stacey did her make-up in smoky eyes.

Ashanti had chosen to wear skinny distressed-hemmed jeans in Ontario wash. She added a burnt-orange, tiered tank top to wear under her boxy-cut denim jacket. She finished her outfit with brown 3" pumps.

The pep-rally was truly exciting. "Finesse" by Bruno Mars and Cardi B was playing as the students entered the gym. Chris has been drawn to escort Stockard. Ashanti was escorted by Dimitri Barnes, the star running back for the Stallions.

Stockard had increased her visits to her therapist in preparation for the day. Her therapist encouraged her to use the mantras she had been given. She also suggested adding beads to help her with her anxiety. Stockard decided on a lapis-luzil anti-anxiety bracelet as an accessory. She wore dangling earrings with the same stones. She rubbed the beads on her bracelet whenever she felt a panic attack coming on. It worked as she walked into the gym.

As her name was being called, she slid to the edge of her chair and rose to her feet. Stockard counted to ten as she waited for Chris to offer his right arm to escort her to the Stallion emblem in the center of the court then back to her seat. She remembered to place one foot in front of the other as she walked to the center. She was happy the earrings bounced against her upper jaw to reminder her to take deep breathes and keep calm.

The remainder of the junior, sophomore, and freshman courts were called. Students casted their votes on either their cell phones or the computers in the atrium to the gym. Eastridge Stallions listened to "Call Out My Name" by the Weekend as they casted their votes and exited the gym.

Chris escorted Stockard to Ashanti's car, "I hope to see Miss "Somebody" at The Lake after the game," he said casting her a smile as he left for the locker room.

"Dimitri didn't walk me to my car," Ashanti said as Chris walked away. "What's that all about?"

"I don't know," Stockard replied. "I guess he was just being a good escort."

✳✳✳✳✳✳✳✳✳✳✳✳✳✳✳✳✳✳✳✳✳✳✳✳✳✳✳✳✳✳✳✳✳✳✳✳✳✳✳✳✳✳✳✳✳✳✳✳✳✳✳

The crew was waiting at the Nicolette house when the young ladies arrived. The crew consisted of Stacey, Raven, and Raven's younger sister Jade; Mrs. Bailey, Aunt Dionne, and Ashanti's cousins; and Stockard's mother, brother, and grandmother.

"Pizza's on the way," Michael announced as he ran up the stairs into his bedroom. "Jeff is coming over, too. He's going to game with us," he added, addressing his mother.

The girls followed Michael upstairs.

"Can you believe the Class of '95 painted the rock?" Stockard asked the group.

"I heard they raised the most money for the Technology Scholarship this year," Raven answered.

"What's the Technology Scholarship?" Stockard probed.

"The Technology Scholarship is the money used to purchase a MacBook, iPad, and iPhone to give to a student or two going to college. The class that raised the most money gets to paint the rock for homecoming," Raven described. "Apparently, the Class of '95 raised the most money this year."

"That's cool!" Ashanti, Stockard, and Jade expressed in unison.

Stockard and Ashanti emerged from their "dressing rooms" soon after Stacey, Raven, and Jade had worked their magic. Jade was chosen as make-up artist because she was great with creating dramatic eyes, something the girls would need on the football field. Jade demonstrated a few dance moves as she created her signature looks. She swayed her legs, popped her arms, arched her back, and did spin moves to help energize the moment to "Party" by Chris Brown. Jade pulled up "All

Eyes on You" after she had worked her magic. She wanted to send Stockard and Ashanti downstairs in style.

"The dress looks better on you than it did in the picture," Mrs. Bailey complimented her granddaughter.

"Thank you, grandma," Ashanti replied. She gave her grandmother a hug, a hug she wished she could have given her mother.

"You look beautiful, 'Shanti," Aunt Dionne stated. "I know Larissa would be proud." She reached for her niece and gave her a hug.

Ashanti's cousins looked up at her with glowing eyes. "You look pretty 'Shanti," Marcus said.

The Bailey family was admiring the crimson colored dress with capped sleeves. The bodice had a two-tone neckline with a lace pattern that joined the skirt with a mock cut-out at the waistline. The skirt had boxed pleats that landed just above Ashanti's knees. Ashanti felt the dress gave her the pizazz she wanted while pleasing her grandmother.

"Here comes Stockard," Michael announced from the top of stairs. That was his way of letting everyone know what he thought about his sister's appearance.

"Does she look pretty?" his mother asked.

"I guess," he replied before retreating to his room to rejoin his guest.

Stockard strolled down the stairs with Stacey and Raven following her. Stockard had chosen an emerald colored, boat neck dress. The bodice had capped sleeves with beaded and jeweled geometric patterns that glistened in the light. Stacey thought the dress would help Stockard sparkle under the stadium lights. The skirt was an inch above her knees and made of tulle. She wore 3.5" inch decorative stilettos to give herself a little more height.

Stacey had twisted Stockard's curls into a bun. She accented her hair with pins similar to the jewels in her bodice. Her dangling earrings matched the emerald and silver beaded bracelet on her right wrist. Jade chose to design Arabic eyes with jade, gold, black, and bronze shadows. Jade told Stacey and Raven that Stockard's face was any make-up artist's dream canvas.

Stockard turned in the direction of her mother and grandmother. The expressions on their faces read they were pleased with what they saw. Stockard had worried that her grandmother would be a little upset at her "showing too much skin" in the Fall. She was aware of her grandmother's conservatism, which is why she chose a dress she thought would satisfy her grandmother while allowing her to assert her personality.

**********************************************

The lights on the 50-yard line were a lot brighter than they were between the 25th and 15th yard lines where the cheerleaders entertained the home crowd. The illumination made Stockard nervous. The lights were blinding when looking into the stands. She decided to focus her attention on the area between the field and the first row of seats. She looked to her left and could see that Thai'ziah would be her escort. She began taking deep breathes to calm her anxiety. She slightly moved her head to feel the earrings against her jaw.

Stockard's name was called along with the names of her football and JROTC escorts. She walked to the appointed spot on the field, counted to ten, then allowed Thai'Ziah to lead her to their left. Stockard was happy to know that Ashanti would be standing next to her in approximately forty-five seconds. Only one name was left in the junior class after Ashanti made it to her spot on the field.

"It's really bright out here," Ashanti whispered to Stockard.

Stockard turned her head slightly to the right to advance her vision towards Ashanti. She was astonished to see the look on Javaris's face. *He was definitely talking to Ashanti that day in the hall. She just didn't realize it*, she thought to herself.

"I never knew how bright it was on the field. Standing down there," she motioned towards the cheerleaders, "is not this bright," Stockard said feeling a bit exposed.

Stockard told herself to keep calm. She reminded herself that one day she may be on stage or in movies, so this was a perfect time to practice. *You do this every Friday night, so you've got this. Count to ten; count to ten.*" She had gotten so lost in her thoughts to remain calm that she didn't realize the entire court had been called. It wasn't until one of her fellow cheerleaders walk to the center of the field to be crowned Miss Crimson and Silver that she focused on what was happening on the field. A member of the senior court walked to the center of the field to receive the Miss Crimson and Gold title.

"Miss Stallion goes to Stockard Nicolette!" the commentator announced. Thai'Ziah had to use a little muscle to get her to move. Stockard was awestruck with the announcement!

Stockard joined the other winners in the designated area for pictures when they left the field. This was the first time she had received such individualized attention. Her palms were becoming sweaty. She rubbed her bracelet and moved her to head to get her earrings to bounce against her jaw.

At thought crossed her mind. Could she be feeling joy at having this much attention? She liked the attention while at the same time wanting her privacy. She enjoyed being in her shell, or so she thought. All her mixed feelings were causing her to feel a panic attack. She took deep breathes to calm her anxiety.

\*\*\*\*\*\*\*\*\*\*\*\*\*\*\*\*\*\*\*\*\*\*\*\*\*\*\*\*\*\*\*\*\*\*\*\*\*\*\*\*\*\*\*\*\*\*\*\*\*\*\*\*

The Homecoming After Party for juniors and seniors was always held at Boyd Park, a tradition that had been in place since the 1980's. The park had the perfect amenities – clubhouse, covered shelters, lake access, and plenty of parking. Homecoming winners received a limousine ride to The Lake sponsored by members of the alumni club. Stockard had not mentally prepared herself for the possibility of being crowned one of Eastridge's princesses. She decided to dig in deep and display the excitement all the other winners were showing. There was no reason to break tradition.

When Stockard stepped out of the limousine, she could tell many of the party-goers had missed at least half of the game. Leaving at half-time was completely understandable because Eastridge was leading by 21 points. It would have taken a miracle for Nations Ford to come back on the Stallions.

Stockard walked up to the clubhouse with Casey and Robin, two of the other winners. They were met with congratulations and hugs as they followed the pathway to the entrance.

The usual spread of food was situated in the far-right corner. Stockard wanted to make her way there for comfort. Her weight was something she struggled with because food, especially cheese, provided her comfort. She was happy to see mini pizzas. She knew she could get her cheese fix on with those.

Just as she was about the make her way to the food, Thai'Ziah came behind Stockard and tapped her on the back.

"Congratulations!" he said. "You didn't even know your name was called, girl," he laughed. "I almost had to drag you from your spot to get you to move," he continued still laughing.

"I'm sorry," Stockard apologized. "I had no idea my name would be called. It's just that the lights were extremely bright out there. It's not the same when you are on the sidelines."

"I feel you on that," he agreed. "Where's your girl at?" he asked inquiring about Ashanti while searching the room for her.

"She's on her way. The homecoming winners came here in a limo, so we couldn't ride together."

"Ooohh, so you got a limo ride tonight?" he half asked and half stated. "That's what's up!" he continued as he balled his hand into a fist and brought it to his mouth while tilting his head back.

"Yeah, it was pretty cool," she responded with her mischievous smile that was rarely seen.

"I'm gonna have to watch out for you, girl. You're not the same person you are when we're at school," he said. He admired Stockard from the tip of her head to the stilettos that gave her height.

"It's a party, right? Can a girl let it down a little bit?" Stockard shocked herself by talking to Thai this way. She was not sure where this side of her was coming from. A part of her was feeling a little flirtatious. She decided to just go with the moment.

"Your girl just walked in the room," Thai informed her by motioning his head in the direction of the door.

Stockard looked in Ashanti's direction and waved. Her friend waved back with a wink. Ashanti made her way to Stockard and Thai.

"Congratulations!" Ashanti said to Stockard while giving her a hug. "How do you feel?"

"I'm excited," Stockard answered embracing Ashanti back. She was displaying the same mischievous smile Thai had received.

"Good," Ashanti said with another wink. Realizing it was rarely Stockard spent time with members of the opposite sex, Ashanti said, "I'll talk to you later."

Stockard was so focused on her college goals that boys and a romantic relationship were not things she entertained on a regular basis. Parties were not something she attended. She fantasized about what it would be like having a relationship in college but never had the thought crossed her mind about high school.

"I'm going to get something to eat," Stockard said to Thai.

"I'll go with you," he said turning in the direction of the food table.

Stockard was not sure this was something she had signed up for. She didn't know what she would talk about if Thai continued to accompany her for the rest of the night.

Stockard was happy to see the mozzarella sticks on the table. Pizza was fine, but mozzarella was pure cheese.

A huge "Heeeyyyy," increased the noise level in the room. Stockard and Thai turned in the direction of the roar to see some of the football team coming through the door. The energy in the room increased 100 times. The volume coming through the speakers seemed to triple as space was created for the dancefloor.

"I'm the One" was next on the playlist. The dancefloor was flooded with people singing and drowning out DJ Khaled. Arms were raised in the air to the words, "I'm the one, yeah, I'm the one." Watching her peers on the dancefloor, Stockard spotted Chris pointing to himself. "I'm the one that hit that same spot," he was singing.

Stockard found herself dancing in place when Calvin Harris's "Slide" shuffled its way onto the speakers. She felt alive and invigorated. She didn't need the cheese like she thought.

"Get it shorty," a voice from behind Stockard spoke in her ear.

She turned in the direction of what was meant to be a whisper as she realized what she was doing. Her dancing was just as spontaneous as shaking her legs and palms sweating. She noticed the eyes that had landed on her as she began to feel somewhat uncomfortable yet intrigued by the attention.

"By the way, congratulations on winning Miss Stallion," Chris said to her in a normal, loud voice.

"Thanks," Stockard said flashing Chris the mischievous smile that had become her signature for the night. "Congratulations to you, too."

"I'm the one that hit that same spot," Chris repeated the words he sang on the dancefloor returning a naughty smile.

"Whaz'up, man," Thai said giving Chris some dap.

"Whaz'up?" Chris responded nodding his head while returning the love.

"Man, you did it out there tonight," Thai said. "You shut that receiver the f," he stopped amid his word, "down. He couldn't do anything tonight because you were on him so tight."

"Hey, that's what I do! Right?" Chris responded with pride and confidence.

Chris was bound by the promises he made to himself while recovering from his injury. He was determined to make this a great year. Last year's injury was a huge set-back for him; it somewhat took him off the radar for possibly making an all-star team.

Chris resolved not to let that get to him too much, even though he struggled with defeating thoughts from time to time. Sho', his personal trainer, did the best he could to help him keep his confidence up. Sho' shared his successes and failures throughout his sports career.

Chris looked to his left and was stunned by the beauty that stood next to him. He knew Stockard was a gorgeous, but he never realized she was a true KNOCKOUT! He wondered why she hid herself behind clothes that really didn't emphasize her body.

So many thoughts ran through his mind. He glanced over at Thai and wondered if his thoughts were invading Thai's space.

*She's fair game,* Chris thought to himself. He cut his eyes over Stockard's head to read Thai. Chris felt he might be invading Thai's space. Consequently, that's what games are about.

"Did either of you see where Ashanti went?" Stockard asked interrupting both of her friends' thoughts.

"I saw her walking towards the lake when I was coming in," Chris answered.

"I think I'll see what's going on by the lake, too," Stockard announced as her exit.

"I can go with you," Thai suggested not wanting to leave her company.

Chris said, "Check you later," to Stockard examining her body one last time. "Ah'ight, man," he said to Thai. Then he made his way towards the dancefloor.

Stockard and Thai walked outside. They stopped to talk with Javaris. He joined them as they walked towards the lake.

"Where's your girl?" Javaris asked Stockard.

"I hope she's by the lake," Stockard answered.

"I hope so, too," Javaris whispered to himself.

They continued to walk towards the lake stopping for Stockard to receive congratulations along the way. Stockard had never received so much attention. She felt overwhelmed. Ashanti being around helped her deal with the attention because she was a natural at working crowds. Stockard had not spotted

Ashanti among the throng of peers, so she decided to walk away from the crowd just to breathe. Thai and Javaris continued to accompany her on the trip.

As Stockard continued her stroll to the lake, she heard what seemed to be a familiar voice. It sounded like Ashanti, yet the speech and laughter were a little slurred. She almost ignored the sounds until she heard the voice say, "Get your hands from under my dress!"

Stockard quickened her pace, trying to find where the voice was coming from. She heard it again, "I said, 'GET YOUR HANDS FROM UNDER MY DRESS!'"

Stockard was in close enough proximity to see a person in the boat slip. Through two planks of wood, she saw two bodies. A person was pulling away from someone else.

"ASHANTI!" Stockard called out to her friend, increasing her pace to the boat slip. "Dang it," she said. Her heel sank into the dirt.

"GET OFF ME!" she heard her friend say again. "STOP! GET OFF ME!"

"ASHANTI!" Stockard repeated in a louder voice.

"What's going on?" Thai and Javaris called out. They were jogging to catch up to Stockard.

Ashanti emerged from the boat slip. She was straightening her dress with one hand and hitting the space behind her with the other.

"Ashanti," Stockard said. "What's going on?"

"Nothing!" Ashanti responded. "I'm ready to go home."

Stockard, Thai, and Javaris marched behind Ashanti as she made her way back to the clubhouse area; she marched directly to the parking lot.

"Thai, Javaris, could you see that Rian and Brenna get home?" Stockard asked trying to keep pace with Ashanti.

"Yeah," Thai said. "I'll give them a ride."

Javaris tried walking with the girls to the parking lot but detected his presence was not wanted. He stood a few feet into the area like a sentinel and watched as they drove away. He remained glued to the spot until he could no longer see their tail lights.

Everything was silent on the way to the Nicolette home. Ashanti made her way to the bathroom. Stockard could hear the shower running. A half hour passed. Another fifteen minutes and no Ashanti. Stockard thought, *That's a long shower.*

After what seemed like an hour, Ashanti appeared from the bathroom to see Stockard sitting on the bed Ashanti had claimed as her own.

"Do you wanna talk about it?" Stockard asked, trying to be a source of comfort.

"I just wanna go to sleep," Ashanti replied. Just as Stockard was rising from her seat, Ashanti said, "Don't say anything to your mom about what happened. I don't want my grandma to know. She has a hard time letting me do anything normal teenagers do. I don't want her freaking out."

"I won't; I promise," Stockard said as she left Ashanti's bedroom.

# Chapter 5

"Hello," Stockard said awakening from her slumber.

"Hey, it's Javaris. I got your number from Thai. I tried to call Ashanti, but she won't answer. What happened last night?" he inquired.

Stockard propped her head on a second pillow as she allowed Javaris's voice and question to wake her up. "I don't know. She didn't say."

Stockard began recalling the last five minutes of the party. She began feeling empathy for her friend.

"I heard her say something about her dress and a hand. I really didn't know anything was going on until

I heard you yell her name. Everything happened so fast," Javaris replied.

"All I know is that I heard her tell somebody to get off her. She came from the boat slip after I called her name. I don't know anything other than that." Stockard decided to keep what she saw to herself.

"Is she okay?" Javaris asked with deep concern.

"I haven't talked to her this morning," Stockard informed. She moved the phone away from her ear to check the time. She couldn't believe it was 8:18. "Why are you up so early?" she inquired.

"I really didn't sleep last night. We stayed out at The Lake until after three. I couldn't sleep thinking about Ashanti," Javaris informed the half-awaken person.

"How did things go?" Stockard questioned.

"Every party is just about the same. People drank a little but that was about it. I just hung out and talked to people. The party was still thumping when I left," he stated.

"I don't do parties like that," Stockard said.

"I know. I was kind of shocked to see you at The Lake last night. I guess winning Miss Stallion was a reason to celebrate," Javaris said trying to sound encouraging.

"I thought it was expected of me, especially since we got a limo ride that brought us straight here. I guess I didn't have much of a choice. I enjoyed myself, a lot," Stockard said feeling elated.

"Do you think Ashanti will mind if I visit her today?" Javaris asked having blocked out Stockard's last comments.

"She spent the night here. I don't know what time she'll go home or if she works today. I'll let her know you called," Stockard said.

"Could you tell her to call me?" Javaris asked, his voice increasing its pitch.

"Okay, I'll do that," Stockard promised.

Stockard went to the bathroom and was surprised to see she still had make-up on her face. She examined her teeth to see if she brushed last night. Negative! She must've been pretty tired.

Stockard heard her mother downstairs talking to Michael. It was too early for Q&A, so she decided to just use the toilet, wash the make-up off her face, and brush her teeth before returning to bed. She was still trying to process what had happened last night and didn't want to answer any questions about the evening.

Stockard loved her mother dearly; nevertheless, she felt her mother was a little too over protective. Her mother had keen senses that she didn't want to deal with until later. She simply wanted to check in on Ashanti before facing her mother.

\*\*\*\*\*\*\*\*\*\*\*\*\*\*\*\*\*\*\*\*\*\*\*\*\*\*\*\*\*\*\*\*\*\*\*\*\*\*\*\*\*\*\*\*\*\*

"What happened last night?" Ashanti asked Stockard as soon as she opened her eyes.

Stockard was dumbfounded to see Ashanti sitting at the foot of her bed. Ashanti was always downstairs with her mother and brother when she spent the night. Stockard was beginning to get a little nervous about the situation because her mother would immediately pick-up on something not being right. She rose up on her elbows to get a clearer view of her friend.

"I'm not sure," Stockard said trying to wake up.

"I think I got drugged last night," Ashanti said.

By that admission, Stockard became fully awake, sitting crossed legged on her bed. She rubbed her hands over her quilt to calm the panic attack that was threatening to take over the moment.

"Why do you say that?" Stockard asked trying to calm her own anxiety. It was instances like these that made her stay away from parties.

"I don't feel right. I have a bad headache, a different headache, one like I've never had before. I drank half a beer before I started to feel funny. Nothing on my body feels right," Ashanti described.

Stockard described to Ashanti what she heard and saw the night before. Tears began to well-up in Ashanti's eyes.

"Who else knows?" Ashanti asked.

"Javaris and Thai were walking with me. We didn't see who was in the boat slip. What do you remember?" Stockard probed.

"I can't remember much of anything!" Ashanti admitted with frustration.

Stockard dropped her head. She searched for words to speak to ease the awkward silence.

"Javaris called this morning. He wants you to call him. He wants to see you," Stockard informed with compassion.

The girls sat in more silence. Stockard didn't know what to say. She changed her position to join Ashanti by the edge of the bed. She grabbed Ashanti's hand and held it.

"I'm here for you," Stockard reassures Ashanti. This was the first time Stockard had viewed herself as the stronger of the two in their friendship. Roles were seeming to change between the friends.

\*\*\*\*\*\*\*\*\*\*\*\*\*\*\*\*\*\*\*\*\*\*\*\*\*\*\*\*\*\*\*\*\*\*\*\*\*\*\*\*\*\*\*\*\*\*

Stockard resolved to face her mother and brother. She walked to the kitchen to eat and take her medicine. A few minutes later, Ashanti joined the Nicolette family. Surprisingly, Stockard was civil towards Michael.

"So how did you feel when they called your name for Miss Stallion?" Michael asked his older sister. "It seemed like Thai had to drag you to the front."

"I was astonished! Okay? I didn't expect to win," Stockard answered Michael with a kind tone.

"What's wrong with you?" Michael asked.

"What do you mean?" Stockard questioned.

"You answered my question without having an attitude," he replied making a face trying to cover up his relief of not being pushed away.

"She just won Miss Stallion, Michael. Isn't that reason enough to be nice to you?" the matriarch interrupted before the usual attitudes and bickering began to ensue.

"Whatever," Stockard replied. She had more important things on her mind. Being aggravated by her little brother was a low priority.

"How was the LIM-O-Zine ride?" Michael continued his questions while making another face.

"It was a limousine ride." Stockard answered, rolling her eyes out of annoyance.

"See, Mama. What I told you. She's always having an attitude with me," Michael began feeling like he was regaining power and getting his old sister back.

"The limousine ride was nice. It carried us directly to The Lake for the afterparty," Stockard answered. She wasn't in the mood for the usual dog-and-cat fight she and Michael had on a daily basis.

"The AFTERparty?" Michael asked.

"Yeah, every homecoming is followed by an after party at Boyd Lake," Stockard offered her little brother, trying on enlighten him to what happens in high school.

Realizing he was not going to get a rise out of his sister, Michael directed his attention to the person in the room he secretly had a crush on.

"Hey, Ashanti," Michael said changing the tone of his voice. "How was the afterparty?" He asked with confidence. He knew a little more about the culture of high school football thanks to Stockard.

Ashanti turned to Michael to answer his question, trying her best to gain the composure she needed to be her usual self. "It was good," she answered.

Her best efforts were not enough to give Michael the attention he was seeking.

"Oh," Michael said, sensing something very different in her. "I'm going outside to get some shots up,"

Michael informed feeling like he had no place in the kitchen. He exited the room to go to his comfort place - his basketball goal.

Having Michael in the kitchen had its benefits for everyone. As soon as he left, the tension in the room increased. Using her motherly instincts, Ms. Nicolette could sense something was awry with Stockard and Ashanti. She didn't quite know what it was. She had once been a teenager and could only imagine the secrets the girls were keeping between them.

*It's not the right time to pry*, the mother thought to herself. *Give them time to work it out. If they need me, they will let me know.*

Stockard knew her mother well. She could feel the vibrations coming from her mother that told her mother's *Spiderwoman* senses were tingling.

Michael burst in the kitchen again announcing, "I forgot to drink some water before I went out. I don't want to catch a cramp." He was still seeking familiar attention from either Stockard or Ashanti.

Stockard wished he would not leave so she wouldn't have to answer her mother's questions. Just as she was pondering what her answers would be, Ms. Nicolette decided to go upstairs.

A wave of solace flushed over the girls. For a moment, Stockard felt like she was having a hot flash.

She realized it was the relief from the panic attack she did not know she was having until it was over.

Michael tried with another question to get Ashanti's attention. "Did you have a good time last night?"

No answer. Ashanti was distant in her thoughts. She didn't even acknowledge him. Not knowing how else to engage Ashanti, Michael said, "Later." He retreated to his basketball goal to ponder what could be the matter with his sister and her friend.

Stockard sat on the barstool next to Ashanti. "My mom knows something is wrong," she advised. "I know her; she's going to ask all sorts of questions about what's going on. It might not be today, but it is coming," Stockard said putting Ashanti on notice.

"I've been trying to remember what happened last night. All I know is that we walked down to the boat slip to drink beer. I don't know what happened after that," Ashanti explained.

"Do you remember walking back to the clubhouse?" Stockard asked.

"No!" Ashanti said in a trembling voice.

"Do you remember driving us home?" Stockard asked.

"No!" Ashanti answered with the same tremble.

"Do you remember taking a shower when you got here?" Stockard probed.

"No," Ashanti replied feeling defeated.

"Do you remember going to bed last night?"

"No," Ashanti answered.

"What do you remember?" Stockard asked.

"Walking to the boat slip then waking up here. When I woke up, things didn't feel right. It's like I have a gap in time. I've had beer before, and it has never made me feel like this. I didn't even have that much. Something bad happened to me last night, Stockard!" Ashanti said. Tears were streaming down her face. Ashanti felt numb.

"Who went to the boat slip with you?" Stockard asked.

"Zoe, Carlie, Seth, Kevin, Jamie, and Rian. We went to just hang-out," Ashanti answered.

"Who brought the beer?" Stockard asked.

"It was already there in a cooler when we got there. That's why we went to the boat slip in the first place. Everybody knows beer is in a cooler by the boat slip. I never asked who brought it," Ashanti said.

"Why did everybody leave?" Stockard questioned

"That's what I don't remember. I don't even remember anyone leaving," she answered staring off into the distance.

Feeling powerless, Stockard said, "You probably need some sleep. Do you have to work today?"

"Not really; I'll call my uncle and let him know I can't make it today. He said it was no big deal if I wanted to stay home. I just needed to let him know," Ashanti informed.

"Yeah; I think that's a good idea," Stockard agreed.

"I'll call when I get upstairs," Ashanti said leaving the room.

"I'll try to keep Michael away from you today," Stockard said.

"He's okay," Ashanti said. "He's a cool person."

"He can be annoying at times," Stockard said.

"He's doing what little brothers are supposed to do," Ashanti said with a slight smile on her face.

That was the first gleam of happiness Stockard had seen in Ashanti all morning. She inhaled deeply, walked to the family room, and struck her warrior pose. Her anxiety levels had increased. Doing a few yoga stretches allowed her to release the tension before it became too intense. She needed to clear her mind.

While in her yoga poses, she realized how much stress last night had really caused her. Likewise, she was feeling a bit empowered. Stockard had not entered the flight mode that used to be her reaction in social situations like last night's party. There was a time when she wouldn't even consider going to The Lake. Reflections on last night made her appreciate being a teenager and Miss Stallion. She was not sure what that title meant in the long run. Would she be expected to attend more parties? She promised herself that she would do her best to enjoy the honor.

Stockard turned her head down to the left while in her side angle pose to her ringing phone. She recognized the number from earlier in the morning. It was Javaris. She exited her pose to answer the call.

"Hello," Stockard answered.

"Hey," Javaris answered back. Silence. "How's Ashanti doing?" he inquired.

"Sleeping," Stockard answered. She had assumed a stork pose.

"Still sleeping?" Javaris asked in astonishment.

"She had breakfast then went back to the bed," Stockard informed him.

"So, what happened?" Javaris asked.

"She doesn't remember anything. Have YOU heard anything?" Stockard asked.

"Nobody has said anything about *that* from last night," Javaris informed. "I don't think anybody knows."

"I hope it stays that way. What happened last night is something that is very difficult for girls to deal with," Stockard said.

"Yeah, I know." Javaris answered. Silence.

"Can I come over later?" Javaris asked. "I want to make sure she's okay," he said.

"Yeah, I'll let her know," Stockard said, hoping Ashanti would be okay with company.

"What time can I come?" Javaris asked.

"After 2:00. Okay?" Stockard replied.

"Yeah, see you then." Javaris said.

\*\*\*\*\*\*\*\*\*\*\*\*\*\*\*\*\*\*\*\*\*\*\*\*\*\*\*\*\*\*\*\*\*\*\*\*\*\*\*\*\*\*\*\*\*\*\*\*\*\*\*\*\*

Two o'clock must have been ten minutes away or time quadrupled its pace. It seemed like Stockard had been off the phone for only a few minutes before Javaris came over. She was glad her mother had errands to run and had insisted that Michael go with her. Ashanti joined Stockard and Javaris in the family room.

"Hey, I was worried about you and wanted to stop in to check on you," Javaris said to Ashanti.

"Thanks," Ashanti stated.

No one knew what to talk about. The awkwardness from the previous night plagued the minds of the teenagers and the room with silence.

"Stockard, let's finish watching 13 Reasons Why," Ashanti suggested, breaking the silence.

The request startled Stockard. Javaris looked at Stockard and shrugged his shoulders. He didn't know what to say. "Do you really want to watch that?" Stockard asked.

"Yeah, Michael's not here, so we don't have to worry about him coming into the room," Ashanti said.

When Stacey and Raven carried the girls shopping for Homecoming, they introduced the family to the series. Ms. Nicolette was uncomfortable with Michael watching the show because of the issues that it raised. Stacey and Raven convinced her that he needed to understand some of the problems he could face in high school.

Apprehensively, Stockard turned on the television, logged-in to Netflix, and tuned in to the next episode in the season. She was a bit perplexed as to why Ashanti wanted to watch the show. 13 Reasons Why could be a trigger for her.

They were able to get through two episodes before Michael returned with his mother. He came into the room just as the episode was ending.

"Did I miss <u>13 Reasons Why</u>?" he asked.

"We just finished the next to the last episode," Stockard answered.

Deepening his voice, Michael asked, "Who are you?" turning to face Javaris with his question.

Javaris introduced himself. Michael walked over and shook his hand. This was one of those lessons he learned from his dad about being man.

What's on next?" Michael asked facing Stockard.

"Which college football game should we turn to?" she asked.

"Turn to the South Carolina/Georgia game," Michael instructed. He bled garnet and black. He had hopes of becoming a Gamecock one day.

Michael knew football very well. He settled into his usual football mode – calling plays, critiquing moves, and scolding referees. Javaris was impressed with the depth of knowledge Michael had about the sport.

"You would make a good announcer," Javaris said to Michael. "You really know your stuff," he added.

Michael looked towards Javaris and nodded his head in agreement. Having Michael around had its benefits, Stockard admitted to herself. He was comfortable in almost every situation. His presence always lightened up the room. Today he was needed more than ever. *Little brothers aren't so bad after all,* Stockard thought to herself.

# Chapter 6

The remainder of the semester was uneventful. The Stallions advanced to the 6-A state championship but lost to a long-time rival, the Bruins. The usual holiday party to celebrate the end of the semester and the Stallion football season was held at The Lake. Ashanti was not interested in the party. Stockard went for a couple of hours with Javaris, Thai, and a few other friends.

Javaris was becoming a close friend since he had been spending so much time around Ashanti. Michael enjoyed having him around. It was like having a big brother. The only time Michael had a problem with Javaris being around was when he saw Javaris looking at Ashanti. Secretly, Michael knew that Ashanti only thought of him like a little brother, but that didn't do much to help the crush he had on her.

Michael was still a little concerned about Ashanti. Things had changed with her since homecoming. He really wanted his bubbly friend back. All of this was confusing to him. He often thought about Hannah from <u>13 Reasons Why</u> when he saw how sad Ashanti got from time to time.

Another body had begun to spend time around the Nicolette home. Chris first came when he brought Javaris over when his car was broken. Then he started to come just to hang-out. Michael didn't mind having Chris around. He admired Chris's talent and followed him on social media and MaxPreps. Michael could recall Chris's stats quicker than he could.

"I told you the boy's a sports genius," Javaris told Chris right after the playoffs had ended. "He could call some plays for you."

Michael enjoyed watching football and basketball with people who could engage in a conversation. His mother tried, but it was not her thing. Stockard would give him about an hour before she retreated to her room. The testosterone was welcomed!

Ms. Nicolette was not sure what was going on with the extra bodies in her home. Things had changed quite a bit since homecoming. She assumed that the girls were dating, or the guys were trying to get their attention.

Ashanti had insisted on finishing the last two episodes of 13 Reasons Why. Then she started watching Pretty Little Liars.

Just before Winter Break was over, Ashanti seemed even sadder. Holidays are always difficult for people living with depression. Even if Ashanti did not have an official diagnosis, everyone around her knew she must be struggle with it to some degree.

While helping Ashanti through this difficult time, Stockard began to understand what it must be like for her mother and brother to live with her depression. Her appreciation of her grandmother increased, too. It was her grandmother who provided the extra support for the family during times of emotional crisis. Seeing herself in Ashanti made her want to work harder on overcoming her depression.

\*\*\*\*\*\*\*\*\*\*\*\*\*\*\*\*\*\*\*\*\*\*\*\*\*\*\*\*\*\*\*\*\*\*\*\*\*\*\*\*\*\*\*\*\*\*\*\*\*\*\*

It was three days before the eve of New Year's Eve when Stockard heard her mother downstairs in the wee hours of the morning. She went to the kitchen to see what was going on. She was not expecting to see her Aunt Lenora, Ashanti, and Mrs. Bailey. Moreover, she was shocked to see Ashanti without her body wave.

"I don't think you should wait to carry her to the pediatrician," Aunt Lenora was saying. "She needs to go somewhere tonight. If she's been cutting herself on her stomach and cut her hair tonight, she needs immediate help."

Those words awakened Stockard even more. She understood all too well what was going on. *Ashanti didn't tell me she had been cutting herself,* Stockard thought; *things must be worse than she pretends like they are.*

"Ashanti, are you okay?" Stockard asked.

Ashanti looked up with a weary face. Stockard walked over to her. She could read the expression on her face. She instantly knew her friend needed her. Silent tears rolled down Ashanti's numbed face. Stockard could only imagine what was going through her friend's mind if she was even thinking. Stockard was having trouble containing her own thoughts. Thoughts of her own emotional pain crossed her mind. Stockard couldn't speak. Seeing Ashanti like this was taking Stockard into her own emotional abyss. Seeing Ashanti like this increased the connection Stockard had with her friend.

"I never had to deal with anything like this before," Mrs. Bailey said. "I don't know what's wrong with her. She just changed."

"She's been through a lot," Aunt Lenora reminded Mrs. Bailey. "I know we think that when a child loses its mother that they get over it. It takes time. Grief is a long process. Kids are resilient, but they still go through. They have so much to deal with these days," Aunt Lenora tried to explain while providing comfort to the grandmother.

"We didn't have to worry about the things they worry about. These phones," Aunt Lenora held her phone in her hand then began pretending she was texting, "cause a whole lot of problems for kids. Then you have those reality shows that don't show what's really going on in the person's life. Kids believe that stuff, and it gets to the them. She might even be going through something she hasn't' talked about."

"Now remember," Aunt Lenora continued, "she's been through a lot over the years."

"She'll be alright," Jeanie interjected, trying to comfort Mrs. Bailey, too. She knew things couldn't be easy for the grandmother. She also knew that life could get a little worse for her, too.

"I just don't understand how I let her get this far. Did you see anything, Jeanie?" she asked directing her question to Ms. Nicolette.

"I could see a change in her after homecoming. We talked about it and decided to watch for signs of danger. We thought it was the blues because Larissa's not here," Ms. Nicolette reminded the grandmother.

"She seemed to be okay after a while," Mrs. Bailey said.

"She was never the same person after homecoming." Jeanie said. Turning to her daughter, she asked. "What happened at The Lake?"

Stockard looked down at Ashanti and said, "I have to tell them." Stockard retold the story about the boat slip. She was thankful her mother never asked her about that night before now. If she had, Stockard would have lied to protect her friend. She decided to tell the entire truth, beer included. Her friend was in bad shape.

"It's not just that," Ashanti said. "It's everything."

"Everything like what?" her grandmother questioned.

"It's everything, Grandma." Ashanti said in an exhausted tone. "I miss my mama." Tears. "I don't see my dad and brothers." Tears. "Life is just too much." Tears.

"Why didn't you tell me?" the grandmother asked. "I would've helped you."

"I tried to handle everything on my own. I didn't want to worry you," Ashanti informed. "That's why I've been spending so much time over here. I tried not to think about it. I thought I could forget about everything. You don't need to be worried about me."

"You're my granddaughter. I'm supposed to worry about you," Mrs. Bailey said. "That's what grandmothers do – help out when we are needed and worry about grandchildren," the elder lady insisted.

"You don't need to be worried about me," Ashanti stated lethargically. The child was exhausted!

"She needs to go somewhere tonight. Medication will help her get through some of this. Hospitals usually keep people three days for observation then make a decision after that," Aunt Lenora informed Mrs. Bailey. "She'll be alright. Be glad you saw her before things got worse."

Turning to Ashanti, Aunt Lenora asked, "What were you thinking about when you cut your hair?"

Ashanti thought for a moment. She then said, "I was thinking that I would be better off with my mama."

A wave of sympathy and empathy swept through the room. Everyone present wanted to help the child get through this moment.

"What made you cut your hair instead of your stomach this time?" Aunt Lenora questioned.

"I thought I didn't want to live anymore. So, I started cutting my hair. Then something came over me and made me snap out of the fog I was in," Ashanti described to the people in the room. "I felt like I just wanted to stop hurting. I want to live. I just don't want to feel this way anymore; it's too hard," Ashanti answered.

"That's how depression makes you feel," Aunt Lenora said.

Stockard felt so much empathy for her friend. She had been there so many times. Stockard never wanted to hurt her mother, brother, and grandmother. That's why she says her mantras. Therapy and medication help. Life can be overwhelming at times.

\*\*\*\*\*\*\*\*\*\*\*\*\*\*\*\*\*\*\*\*\*\*\*\*\*\*\*\*\*\*\*\*\*\*\*\*\*\*\*\*\*\*\*\*\*\*\*\*

Ashanti's stay at Behavioral Health was less than forty-eight hours. She was released with medications and a follow-up appointment with an out-patient psychiatrist. Mrs. Bailey was told that her granddaughter would be better off at home with the support of her family. The psychiatrist believed that staying in the hospital longer would be more of an adverse experience for Ashanti.

Stockard shared with Ashanti her secret of being on medication to control her anxiety and depression. "You're not the only one, Ashanti." Stockard said trying to let her friend know she understood what she had been going through.

"Why didn't you tell me?" Ashanti asked.

"I told you that I see a therapist," Stockard reminded her.

"You never told me that you take medication," Ashanti said.

"I didn't know how you would feel about me," Stockard admitted.

"I've been on medication since middle school. I try to keep a consistent schedule of taking my medication by 8:00 every morning. That's why I get up on Saturdays then go back to bed after breakfast," Stockard told her friend.

"I thought you were taking vitamins," Ashanti said.

"I take vitamins, too," Stockard affirmed.

"Why didn't you tell me?" Ashanti asked again.

"You know how kids at school are about stuff like this. People call you weak if they know you take psychotropic medications," Stockard began.

"What?" Ashanti asked.

"Mental health medications," Stockard clarified. "Think about what people say about the 'tree' people. Could you imagine what the kids would say to and about me, a cheerleader?" Stockard continued her explanation.

"When I hear kids tease people at school, I'm glad nobody knows! Kids say cruel things when they know someone is going to the school therapist. It's so sad that people can't get the help they need," Stockard spoke her conscious.

"Smoking pot and popping pills is the way to deal with everything. Therapy and prescription medications are not acceptable," Stockard reminded her friend with a firm voice.

"I'm sorry," Ashanti said. "You are right. Kids can be cruel."

Ashanti began thinking about her own feelings about her situations. She felt like the weight of the world was on her shoulders. Sometimes she felt that way when her mother was alive. She often got depressed thinking about what life would be like when her mother was gone. She never imagined it would be this difficult.

\*\*\*\*\*\*\*\*\*\*\*\*\*\*\*\*\*\*\*\*\*\*\*\*\*\*\*\*\*\*\*\*\*\*\*\*\*\*\*\*\*\*\*\*\*\*\*\*\*

Stacey was the best cousin ever. She always knew when she was needed. She and Raven planned the perfect New Year's Eve to help take everyone's mind off things. They reserved bowling lanes in the Epicentre. Plans for the evening surrounded their lane time.

*First Night* had been a tradition in Stockard's family. Raven had joined the family when she was a sophomore in high school. Stacey felt obligated to relieve her aunt of having to maintain the tradition. Stacey thought the middle schoolers, Michael and Jade, might enjoy the experience of feeling like big kids.

Stacey and Raven explained their plans. The only problem Ms. Nicolette had with the idea was the possibility that Stockard would have a panic attack and want to leave earlier than planned.

"Aunt Jeanie, she's going to have to learn to make adjustments around different social situations," Stacey advised. "She will be going to college in less than two years. If she's not going to learn now, when will she learn?" Stacey asked trying to get her aunt to see the importance getting used to Stockard being independent.

Stacey was thinking that her aunt could use the break for all the holiday excitement, too.

"I don't want to ruin everybody else's evening," her aunt answered.

"You didn't think she would be okay for homecoming. Remember? She did just fine. She's even grown up a little since then. You can't keep her protected her entire life, Auntie," Stacey said trying to reason with her aunt.

"I'm just not sure," Aunt Jeanie replied.

"Sure of what?" Stacey asked.

"Sure that Stockard will be okay among all those people," Aunt Jeanie answered.

"We won't be too far away," Stacey said.

"What time are you going to the Westin, again?" Aunt Jeanie asked.

"The party we are going to begins around 11:30," Stacey said. She decided to review the plans again for her aunt's comfort. "We're going to walk them back to the light rail around 11:00. We won't leave until they get on the train. They will park at the I-485 station to avoid a lot of uptown traffic. We are talking 485 and 77, which won't be too bad before 12:30," Stacey said.

"It's all planned out, right?" Aunt Jeanie asked.

"They will be fine. Let them grow up a little," Raven interjected. "My mom's okay with Jade going."

Ms. Nicolette agreed to allow the children to enjoy their first *First Night* without her since Stockard was two years-old. She was feeling lonely and not needed. She wondered how she would spend *her* first night.

Plans were adjusted when Chris and Javaris decided to join the outing. Javaris would use his father's SUV so that everyone would be in the same vehicle. Having the young men around eased some of Ms. Nicolette's concerns for the children. She felt like the girls would be more protected with their friends around.

\*\*\*\*\*\*\*\*\*\*\*\*\*\*\*\*\*\*\*\*\*\*\*\*\*\*\*\*\*\*\*\*\*\*\*\*\*\*\*\*\*\*\*\*\*\*\*

The New Year's Eve outing began with a trip to the ice rink. Since this was Jade's first time on ice, Michael and Raven teamed up to help her. Someone was beginning to steal his heart away from Ashanti.

Javaris was trying his best to get close to Ashanti, the girl he liked since middle school. He skated backwards several times to talk to her about the holidays. Javaris had given Ashanti a pair of hoops that she was wearing. He admired his gift and the girl wearing them.

Chris skated close to Stockard. Having mustered up the courage, he asked Stockard to be his girlfriend. This came as a surprise to Stockard. She thought of Chris more as a friend. They had exchanged Christmas gifts; however, Stockard never imagined it was a gesture indicating Chris wanted to be more than friends. Stockard didn't give him an answer. She needed time to think about it.

When they arrived at Strike City, Stockard took the chance to go to the restroom with Raven. She told Raven about Chris asking her to be his girlfriend. Raven used the occasion to school Stockard on a few facts about boys.

1.  Boys don't hang around unless they are wanting something. "Boys are not trying to *just* be your friend. Remember that!"
2.  If a girl wants to know whether a boy is worth her time, she simply looks at his extracurricular activities. "He's working hard on the football and track fields, which means he's not getting into too much trouble."
3.  A guy with goals who actively pursues them is worth spending time with. "He

is trying to get a football scholarship to a D-1 school. If it's not football, it's track. Every day he's putting forth effort to achieve his goals."

4. Pay attention to the people he considers his friends and confidants. "Javaris is going to the Air Force, so he won't be doing anything to upset his daddy and jeopardize his future."

5. "I came across a quote that read, 'If you can't build with him, you don't chill with him.' You have dreams. He doesn't try to keep you from achieving your goals, making your dreams come true."

"All of that seems logical when I'm ready to get married. I'm just talking about dating right now," Stockard clarified.

"You are not the type of girl guys *just* date, Honey. Guys pick and choose who they date and for what reason. If he asked you out, he has feelings for you." Raven titled her head and said, "I would say, 'Date him.'"

Stockard smiled, "Thanks for the advice." She felt relief getting Raven's approval.

"Oh, the goodies stay in the jar," Raven added as Stockard was pulling the door handle to leave.

Michael and Jade had taken the initiative to enter everyone's name in the lane. Since Stockard was not there when the line-up started, she was last to bowl. Drink orders had been taken. Michael order a Mist Twist for his sister.

The lanes had been rented for two hours. All minors had to leave the establishment by 10:00 to prepare for the New Year's Eve Party for adults.

Between food and bowling, they were able to get through two games. Javaris was the winner of both games. His secret weapon was his dad. Javaris's dad used to play in a league and taught his son techniques when he was younger.

"Quin used to go bowling with us when we were in elementary school," Javaris said remembering his friend. Javaris and Quin lost interest after sixth grade.

Stacey and Raven escorted the group to another concert area before walking to the Convention Center light rail stop. "Call us when you get home," they both said as they made their way to the Westin.

Everyone naturally pair-up on the platform. The wait was filled with chatter from Michael and Jade. They recalled some of Jade's falls while skating. Michael accused Javaris of cheating at bowling because no one knew he had been coached by his dad. Michael and Jade checked their social media accounts to see what their friends were doing to bring in 2018.

Stockard had not given Chris an answer, but that didn't stop him from acting like she had. He sat close to her trying to keep her warm. He reached for her hand to examine the bracelet he gave her for Christmas. Stockard was wanting to give Chris a "yes" but was still a little apprehensive.

Javaris was still acting as if he was Ashanti's protector. He made her smile a few times. Stockard was happy that her friend was enjoying herself.

While on the train, they noticed that adults with children were going south while adults without children were going north. From time to time, Ashanti leaned over to Stockard to whisper a critique of an outfit of a partygoer. Stockard was happy for the interaction. That was the Ashanti she knew and loved.

# Chapter 7

All juniors at Eastridge High School were excited to return for their second semester. Many New Year's Resolutions were centered around losing weight, getting in shape, and having a date for prom.

Stockard and Ashanti were among the girls who decided to join a weight loss challenge in preparation for the big day. They wanted to have the perfect body. The Junior/Senior Prom was the highlight of junior year.

"I ate too many sweets over the holidays," was the most common excuse used to justify needing to join the challenge.

Training for track season intensified in January; therefore, Chris and Javaris did not have to make plans on how they would improve their physique for prom. They both had a goal they wanted to achieve by February 1 – secure their chosen Valentines!

Joyce C. Cooper

# Life Interrupted

## Valentine's Day is Bloody Wednesday

February 14 was supposed to be a special day; a day of love and excitement. Since Eastridge High School had a school policy against sending flowers and other gifts to school, none of girls were expecting gifts until later in the day. Stockard was looking forward to going home and trying on the dress she had bought just for this day.

The dress Stockard had purchased for the night out with her "best guy friend" was the one she had worked eagerly to get into. She joined the weight loss challenge to lose the extra pounds she had put on during the holidays. Her first weight loss milestone was for Valentine's

Day. She was surprised when she realized that she had exceeded her goal!

Stockard was just about to leave her fourth period math class when her cellular phone vibrated with a newsfeed... "Mass shooting at Stoneman Douglas High School in Parkland, FL."

Anxiety, confusion, disbelief! Did she read that correctly? She checked the feed again. There really was another school shooting in America! She walked out of her math class feeling dazed and confused. What if something like that happened at Eastridge? What if something like that happened at her brother's school? She looked up and realized she had walked unconsciously to the edge of the stairwell. Had she waited a second longer, she would've stumbled down the stairs. Her peers filed around her as if they were unaware of what had happened.

A text message from Ashanti vibrated in, "Meet you in the parking lot." Stockard wasn't sure she wanted to go into the parking lot. Although she was being strong for Ashanti, she was still struggling with fear and uncertainty. Despite all that had happened between Homecoming and Winter Break, Stockard felt, that life was a little too hard. She didn't want to kill herself. Some mornings, she simply didn't want to wake up.

One thing that helped her snap out of the feeling was the memory of Crystal. Crystal seemed to have faded from the mind of her peers. Was it just their way of dealing with that painful past? She often wondered what it would be like if she disappeared. Would her mother and brother be able to cope without her? Would her grandmother be able to sleep at nights without tossing and turning in her bed wondering what happened to her beloved granddaughter? It was questions like these that Stockard would not want her family to face. She changed her self-speech, silently repeating her mantra, "I am loved, cherished, and needed."

\*\*\*\*\*\*\*\*\*\*\*\*\*\*\*\*\*\*\*\*\*\*\*\*\*\*\*\*\*\*\*\*\*\*\*\*\*\*\*\*\*\*\*\*\*\*\*\*\*\*\*\*\*\*\*\*\*\*

Stockard turned the television to CNN to get the most up-to-the-minute coverage on the events that happened in Parkland, Florida. She talked to her mom about the things she had on her mind. Thoughts about the school shooting, mental illness, her own thoughts of feeling hopeless and helpless.

Her mother listened without comment. Ms. Nicolette had learned that during times like these, her daughter was simply needing a way to vent her feelings. She no longer tried to help Stockard reason through every negative thought and feeling she had.

"Do you think the person who did this was mentally ill?" she asked her mother. Mental illness was something both she and her mother worked hard to understand. It plagued their family in many ways.

"It is very possible that the person who did this was mentally ill," her mother replied. "Before passing judgment, we need to learn more about what actually happened today."

"Did you have to worry about school shootings when you were in school?" Stockard questioned.

"We had to deal with bomb threats." The mother answered. "I remember having to evacuate the school on several occasions when I was in high school due to bomb threats."

"What happened?" Stockard continued to inquire.

"It was usually some kid who didn't want to go to school." Recalling a high school incident, Mrs. Nicolette said, "I remember a time when we were standing outside for over an hour due to a threat. I was in my physical science class, an outside classroom. When it was time to go back into the school, we heard that someone had made the call from the convenience store two blocks from the school." A smile formed on her face. "Several of us began laughing because we figured the kid's parents must have made him leave the house for school. Bomb threats were a common thing when I was your age. I was happy to be in an outside classroom that time."

"Did it stress you out?" Stockard further questioned.

"I didn't think so then." Looking into the distance, her mother continued. "Now when I that I think about it, yes, it stressed me out. I can remember going to school thinking, *I hope we don't have a bomb threat today.*"

"I always prayed that it was merely a kid who was bluffing because he didn't want to go to school. It took a couple of days for things to settle down after a bomb threat," her mother said.

Stockard tuned in to the television. "The suspect was indeed a student at the school at some point. It seems that he was expelled from the school," a reporter confirmed.

"Expelled!" Stockard repeated. "What did he do?" she continued her conversation with the television.

"You need to get ready for tonight," her mother reminded her.

"I don't really want to go anywhere," Stockard informed her mother. How could she feel safe after all of this?

"You need to go," her mother encouraged her. "You have come a long way. Imagine how good you're going to look in that dress tonight."

Ms. Nicolette desperately wanted her daughter to go on the date with her friend. So much work had been put into her daughter to get her to the point where she could trust someone enough to go on a date, even if it was her "best guy friend."

Stockard's anxiety had not just taken a toll on Stockard's life. It had impacted her brother and mother's lives, too. Helping someone work through anxiety and depression is not an easy feat. It required taking extensive time and energy to listen to what is going on the mind of the person who is suffering. Ms. Nicolette had to be attuned to the signs that might indicate her daughter could be entering crisis mode.

It had been five and a half years since Stockard had been given mental health diagnoses. Ms. Nicolette was determined to help her daughter heal and live a normal life once again.

"It has been confirmed that seventeen people have died at the hands of the gunman," Ms. Nicolette heard the CNN reporter say.

"Seventeen," she whispered to herself in disbelief. "That's a lot of lives lost at the hands of one person." *It's time to do something about these military-grade assault rifles in the hands of civilians,* she thought.

The doorbell ringing made Ms. Nicolette shift her thinking to the safety of her daughter and her date. She strolled to the foyer to open the door and greet the young man who was beginning to grow on her.

Chris's frequent visits to her home and the relationship she was building with his mother helped create trust in him. She opened the door and was greeted with a smiling face and two arms of gifts.

"Hey, Ms. Nicolette," Chris greeted the middle-aged woman.

"Hello, Chris," Ms. Nicolette greeted him back.

"I wanted to get you something for being such a wonderful person," Chris stated as he handed the mother a box of chocolates and a single rose. He stepped into the foyer.

She smiled at the young man as if she was recalling a memory. "Thank you," she said as she gently accepted the gifts. Her eyes twinkled with the recollection of a time long gone.

"Are you okay," he asked the lady, noticing her stare.

She smiled and shared her thoughts. "My most precious Valentine's memory is the year Stockard was a baby. I had come home from work, carrying Stockard in my arms. As I entered the kitchen through the laundry room, I heard Carl Thomas's 'Emotional' blasting through the house. When I reached the kitchen table, it was set with my best dinnerware, flatware, wine glasses, and candles. There was a bear with the year 2001 embroider on a paw sitting in the center of the table."

She paused for just a moment before continuing her story. "The telephone rang just as I was walking through the kitchen. It was from a local restaurant. They were calling to verify exactly how I wanted my prime rib cooked. I knew then what my ex-husband had planned for the evening. He had programmed my favorite slow songs in the cd player and cleaned the house just for me." She smiled. "The best Valentine's Day I ever had. Love at its best," were Ms. Nicolette's last words; the twinkled faded.

The young man could tell that the memory caused her both happiness and sadness. "I could tell that was a good memory for you," he said having a greater appreciation of her life.

Stockard walked into the family room where Chris and her mother were standing. He looked at his girlfriend then extended the candy, a dozen of roses, and card he had put forth a lot of effort in selecting. He wanted to impress her tonight, the girl he considered his girlfriend even though she had not officially said, "Yes."

Chris made special plans for the evening. He was carrying Stockard to her favorite restaurant. Reservations had been made since New Year's Day. He was hoping she would agree to be his girlfriend, his Valentine's by now. Her official "Yes" did not really matter to him. She was acting like his girlfriend.

Ms. Nicolette reached for the remote and turned the television off. She didn't want the traumatizing news of the school shooting to cause her daughter to not enjoy her evening.

She admired her daughter's beauty in the red laced dress she had purchased in an after-Christmas sale two sizes too small. Stockard had vowed to lose weight to get into the dress by Valentine's Day. If she had achieved her goal, then she could go shopping for her prom dress.

\*\*\*\*\*\*\*\*\*\*\*\*\*\*\*\*\*\*\*\*\*\*\*\*\*\*\*\*\*\*\*\*\*\*\*\*\*\*\*\*\*\*\*\*\*\*\*\*\*\*\*\*\*\*\*\*\*\*\*\*

Dinner at Aiazzi's was just what the doctor ordered. Stockard knew Chris was carrying her to dinner. She had no idea he was carrying her to her favorite Italian restaurant. She suspected Michael had leaked the information and even took the initiative to make the reservations.

Chris paid for Valet parking; he didn't want Stockard to walk too far in the February chill. This act alone gave Stockard a new prospective of her "best guy friend." She knew how he was in school and around her home. She had no idea he had as much class as he was displaying.

Stockard and Chris ordered the couple's Valentine's Day special.

They choose stuffed mushrooms for their appetizer followed by Aiazzi's salad, which consisted of mixed greens, crispy prosciutto, red onions, pine nuts, blue cheese, and Aiazzi's house dressing. Stockard ordered a scallop and shrimp combination over orzo pasta, covered with a saffron sauce for her entrée. Chris order veal parmesan as his entrée. The couple agreed on the double chocolate chocolate cake for dessert.

Chris felt so much pride in himself. He had worked in his father's body shop on Wednesdays after school to save money to impress Stockard. His father was not down with giving him the money to finance his son's romances.

Chris typically worked with father on Saturdays to pay for car insurance, gas, and maintenance. His father was determined not to spoil him. He provided only what he and his wife thought were necessities. Chris's father had worked hard to accomplish the things he owned and wanted his son to learn some of the same lessons he had learned growing up.

Stockard enjoyed the ambiance at Aiazzi's. Her first memory of the restaurant was to celebrate her mother's birthday. Many of Stockard's favorite people – Lola, her close friend since toddlerhood and Lola's parents; Aunt Priscilla and Uncle Brian; cousins Chauncy, Stacey and Niecey; and her grandmother – occupied one of Aiazzi's family rooms for the milestone birthday. Every visit to Aiazzi's with Niecey meant an order of stuffed mushrooms.

The distance between Lola and Niecey, who attended South Hill High, and Stockard had increased over the years. Being at different high schools and having different interests was one of the casualties of growing up. Social media feeds were the best way to keep track of friends in the twenty-first century. Being at Aiazzi's made Stockard think of her friends and the times they had been there to celebrate birthdays and other milestone events.

The waitress served the couple their first course. Stockard reached for a mushroom. Before she could get the appetizer, Chris had one on a plate and was serving it to her. She was shocked, in disbelief! She had no idea that guys her age would do something like that. She thought her cousin Chauncy was the "Last of the Mohicans" when it came to chivalry. She thanked Chris for his kindness and waited for him to serve himself.

Chris took his second bite while admiring the loveliness that sat across from him. *If this is a dream, then let me sleep*, he thought.

The couple made small talk throughout the meal. By the time they had completed their entrée, Chris asked her what she thought about the incident in Florida. Stockard didn't want to think it.

Going to school stressed her out every, single day of her life. She had missed several days throughout her middle and high school years due to her anxiety and depression.

Almost once a week, the thought of death crossed her mind. Thinking about what happened to the students in Florida and all the school shootings since elementary school were one reason she felt so much anxiety — the threats of violence and a shooting at a place that was supposed to be a haven.

"It's so sad what happened," Stockard replied. "I just wonder what might have triggered the shooter to do it. The usual report is that the person was bullied at school, but I don't think that's a legitimate reason. Just think about it. Kids are bullied every day in one way or another. That's the way it is."

"You're right," Chris agreed. "When something like that happens, someone has been bullied at school. I was bullied a lot when I was in middle school. I remember staying in my teacher's class in sixth grade because people were wanting me to join a gang. I didn't want to go to lunch or to the bus lot. Eighth graders were making the younger kids join their gang," Chris said.

"One time when I walking to my grandma's house, this dude named Keith ran off a porch and punched me right here in my left jaw," he stated motioning to the spot on his face.

"Are you serious?" Stockard asked furrowing her brow.

"Yeah," Chris said, "but I never thought about killing anybody. That's why I started lifting weights - to protect myself when I went to my grandma's house. I had friends like Julian and Monty when I got there just in case I needed back-up in a fight. They weren't always around to help protect me."

"That must've been difficult. Did Julian and Monty go through the same things?" Stockard asked.

"Julian's dad was not having that, but I think he got caught up a little bit. Monty was not so lucky. He got caught up. That's why he went D-2 instead of D-1. Between his grades and troubles in the neighborhood, D-1 schools were scared when it came to signing him. I guess they didn't want all the baggage. He's on probation now," Chris said.

Chris must've trusted Stockard to share those secrets. Men don't reveal those kinds of things to women, especially his girlfriend. That shows weakness. He was supposed to be strong, her protector. There was something about Stockard that said she was different, could understand what his life was like.

Vulnerability is not something men show. Chris dismissed the thoughts of weakness and returned his attention to the prize sitting in front of him, the heart he was capturing.

"Wow! That's serious stuff," Stockard commented.

"People get bullied every day. I'm sure you've been bullied before in your life," Chris stated.

"All the time," Stockard began. "I remember an incident in elementary school when a group of girls put a spider in my hair. I told my mom about it. When she talked to the principal, she told her it was just girls being girls."

After a brief pause, Stockard continued, "Several times I was bullied by Jason because I wouldn't be his girlfriend. One time he put worms in my desk; another time he took a pack of ketchup and squeezed it on my grilled cheese sandwich. I was so mad at him! Just think; I had to put up with him in middle school, too" she exhaled before going on.

"I was so relieved when he went to South Hill. When he showed up at Eastridge, I wanted to run in another direction. Rumor had it, he left South Hill because he talked too much, and a group of guys were going to jump him," Stockard said.

"I heard that too," Chris confirmed. "I know one of the dudes who was about to jump him."

"Then he transferred to Wesley. Rumor has it he left Wesley because he touched a girl on her breast when they were doing an experiment in chemistry class. He's averaging a high school a year," she laughed.

Stockard looked at Chris, "You didn't ask me for all of that. Did you? You asked me if I had ever been bullied. Yes, I've been bullied. Jason has been my nemesis since elementary school!! I was terrified when I heard him barking in the courtyard just before Homecoming," Stockard admitted, realizing it was her anxiety.

"I heard him and a group of dudes barking in the courtyard one day, too. I was thinking, *I know that dude is not acting like somebody in elementary school. It won't be long before he's kicked out of Eastridge. That guy is bad news*," Chris said.

Their conversation was interrupted by dessert. The waitress brought one dessert and two forks. Apparently, she was unaware of the fact that the two were just friends and not a "real" couple. Her actions were understandable. After all, it was Valentine's Day and only couples would order from the couple's menu.

At first Stockard was a bit apprehensive about sharing the cake with Chris. Although she had accepted his dinner invitation, she had no intentions of allowing him to get close to her.

If they shared cake, he might get the wrong impression. What if their forks accidently hit? Would that mean? What would he think?

She was simply using the date to figure out if she was ready to make being his girlfriend official. If she wasn't, then she should just go to the prom with a group of friends.

After contemplating all the effort Chris had put into the date, Stockard decided it would be okay to share the cake with him.

Their friendship had been building up over the past few months, and she didn't want to lose what they had developed. She was learning how to trust again, and Chris was instrumental in her progression.

"Decadent," Stockard said after she tasted the cake.

"Are you some food expert or something?" Chris asked with a slight snicker. He had never heard anyone use that word.

"I like good food. My family enjoys cooking with fresh ingredients. We grow many of our own herbs. My mom says that cooking relaxes her, which is why we eat at home most of the time," Stockard said.

"My brother and I have been helping her cook every since we were toddlers. She used cooking to help us learn math and how to read. I've been in a kitchen my entire life. If it wasn't with my mother, then it was with my grandmother," Stockard said.

"To answer your question, I consider myself a food connoisseur. Good food means long life," she answered.

"When are you going to cook for me?" Chris asked.

"When would you like for me to?" Stockard questioned.

"How about Saturday?"

"Let me think about it," Stockard answered giving Chris the same playful smile he had seen on Homecoming night.

Chris rubbed his hands over his thighs. He motioned for the waitress to bring the check. He pulled his card from his wallet. He remained silent after he paid the bill. So many thoughts were going through his mind.

Stockard had an idea as to how much the evening had costed Chris. She was very appreciative of all the effort he had placed in making this a special evening. She never imagined that Chris had as much class as he had shown. He was intensifying her feelings for him.

Christ dismissed himself after a few minutes of silence. He looked at Stockard and told her he was going to get the car. He didn't want her to stand in the cold waiting for the car.

Stockard found herself checking Chris out as he walked towards the restaurant's entryway. She was quite impressed with the ribbed, cotton-blend, shawl-neck, allonge sweater Chris was wearing. She never thought any guy at Eastridge would wear anything like that, especially a Stallion. Chris was truly a man of many secrets and secret weapons.

Chris walked out to the valet station and was glad it was parked close to the restaurant's entrance. He looked around the parking lot as the valet took his ticket. He started thinking of how he was going to ask Stockard to the prom. He felt that if he was going to do it, tonight would be the time. He could tell that Stockard enjoyed the evening. She had a glow on her face he had never seen. Watching games with Michael had its benefits.

Spotting the location of his car, Chris returned to the restaurant and walked towards the table he shared with his girlfriend. He was trying to imagine how he could top this for prom.

The ambiance at Aiazzi's was great; he truly understood why it was Stockard's favorite restaurant. The bronze columns with gold accents provided excellent décor. The sconces on the walls and columns provided perfect lighting. No need for candles.

*What are you doing man?* The question crossed his mind. *You don't let a girl do this to you. You never thought about how a restaurant was decorated before tonight,* he thought. What was Stockard doing to him?

Chris smiled at his girlfriend when he reached their table. "The car should be ready when we get outside," he said as he motioned for her to leave.

Watching her rise out of her seat, Chris thought, *She's the most beautiful girl I've ever dated.* Was it her looks or personality or a combination of the two? Her conversation was more enriching than he had ever experienced on a date. It had taken courage and hard work for Chris to get to this point. That's what Stallions do, persevere! The night was worth the struggle.

*********************************************

Little was said between the couple on their ride home. Chris had deviated from his usual Trey Songz playlist. The list he created for the special night softly played through his speakers. He had lowered the bass and increased the treble so that Stockard could clearly hear the instrumentals and words of Usher and Trey Songz. "You Got it Bad" followed by "One Love" then "My Boo" blue toothed from Chris's phone. Perfect timing for the ride home.

"Let your playlist do the talking for you," the guys at Platinum Cuts advised him. He sought their advice when planning the right moves for the girl whose heart he wanted to capture. Chris refused to give a name when asked by the fellas. He only gave a description. If Usher and Trey Songz couldn't get the job done for him, then no artist could.

Stockard was trying to understand her feelings that were developing for Chris. *How do I tell him I will be his girlfriend?* she pondered. *He's doing throw-back*, she thought while enjoying the music. Chris was capturing the attention of the girl he had put so much energy into attracting.

He was feeling a sense of accomplishment. Chris thought he would never get to that night. What would the guys from the football and track teams say when they found out he had taken Stockard on a date? On Valentine's night, he was and was not a Stallion.

When they arrived in Stockard's driveway, Chris had one last move. He swiftly jumped out of the car to open the door for Stockard. He took a deep breath when he was able to reach the passenger side before she stepped out of the car. He smiled down at her and offered his hand; a move Ace told him he should use to end the date.

As soon as Stockard entered the foyer, her phone rang. "How was it?!?" the voice on the other end was asking with such excitement that Stockard was not sure it was a question.

"Let me call you later," she told Ashanti.

Surveying the family room brought Stockard back to reality.

Chris had already taken a seat. Her mother was watching Anderson Cooper on *CNN*. He was sitting in the anchor's chair and interviewing Melissa Falkowski, a teacher at Marjory Stoneman Douglas High School, via satellite.

"We had drilled for this, yes; we had a training recently. We could not have been more prepared for this situation, which makes it so frustrating; 'cause we've trained for this; we've trained the kids for what to do; and so what the frustration is is that we've done everything we were suppose to do; Brevard County School has prepared for this situation; and still, you know, to have so many casualties, ahm, it's, at least for me, it's very emotional. I feel today like, you know, our government, our country has failed us and not kept us safe," Melissa said. As she was talking, two breaking newsfeeds scrolled that read, "SHERIFF: SHOOTING SUSPECT IN CUSTODY" and "SHERIFF: SHOOTING SUSPECT IS EX-STUDENT; HAD ONE AR-15".

Ms. Nicolette reached for the remote and turned down the volume on the television.

"How was dinner?" she asked.

"It was Great!" Stockard answered with so much excitement, she surprised Chris. It had not surprised her mother, though. She knew how much her daughter loved great food, the food at Aiazzi's.

"I'm glad to hear that," her mother responded.

Chris wasn't exactly sure what he should do. He wanted to spend the entire night with the girl who was showing another dimension to her personality, but he didn't want to seem disrespectful by spending too much time with her on a school night.

He looked at the television and read the scrolling newsfeeds. He decided that he needed a little NBA to get him through the night and ready for school tomorrow.

If he left immediately, he could possibly catch some of the Hornets and Magic game. He stood up and rubbed his hands down the sides of his legs.

"I guess I better go," he announced. He looked at Stockard and then her mother then back at his girlfriend. "See you at school tomorrow." He stood to walk towards the door. Ms. Nicolette motioned for Stockard to follow.

Just as Chris was leaving, Michael bounced down the stairs. "How did it go?" he asked the couple.

"Everything was straight," Chris answered Michael.

"Cool," Michael said before returning to his game.

Chris watched Michael leave the room. He turned to Stockard and repeated his previous comment, "See you at school tomorrow."

Stockard followed him to the door. "Thanks, Chris," she said with a twinkle in her eyes that seized his attention. She smiled her flirty smile as she closed the door behind him.

"Good night," Chris said before the door closed behind him. *Was she checking me out?* he thought as he walked to his car. His stomach began to feel a little queasy. "I think she was checking me out," he whispered to himself. *She WAS checking me out!* he finally convinced himself. He felt like a million dollars as he walked to his car. He opened the door, sat in the driver's seat, and looked towards the house. He could swear he saw Stockard looking out the window at him. "She'll go the prom with me," he told himself. Chris was the man!

As he was leaving the driveway, Chris's phone rang. He changed the track coming through his speakers to "Sing Like Me".

*********************************************

Stockard returned the call to Ashanti. "You want to know how it was? It was AMAZING!" she shouted through the phone. "I never knew he had so much class. He shocked me! I have made my decision about prom. If Chris makes an appropriate promposal, I will go with him."

"Are you serious?" Ashanti asked. "Was it that good?"

"Yes!" Stockard describe the evening to her friend. Then she asked the question. "How did he know Aiazzi's is my favorite restaurant?"

"It wasn't me. I bet it was Michael."

"What did you do tonight?" Stockard asked.

"A dozen of roses were waiting for me when I got home," Ashanti shared.

"Tell me more; tell me more," Stockard sang, reclining on the pillows on her bed.

"Yes; with an invitation for dinner!" Ashanti exclaimed.

"And," Stockard said encouraging more conversation.

"So, we had dinner at Fins. How did he know that's my favorite seafood restaurant?" Ashanti questioned.

"He who?" Stockard asked, trying to play dumb.

"Javaris! Who did you think I was talking about?"

"Weelll; he might have overheard me talking about carrying you to your favorite restaurant for your birthday. You know how people make small talk in class," Stockard explained.

Hearing music playing in the background, Stockard asked, "What are you listening to?"

"'I Can't Help But Wait'," Ashanti answered. "He likes Trey Songz," Ashanti continued. "I have it on automatic replay."

"Javaris is really cute. In low lights, his eyes and smile are to diiiiiie for. I have to admit, I was feeling a little guilty about liking him because of Quin. I don't want to break any codes and stuff like that," Ashanti admitted. "Does the bro' code apply?"

"Quin isn't here anymore," Stockard said in a calming voice. "Plus, you and Quin never had *that* kind of a relationship. I don't see that as a betrayal or anything."

"He asked me to the prom, and I said, 'Yes.' I said, 'Yes' because I feel comfortable with him. I was hoping that Chris would ask you. We could all go together," Ashanti said.

"The subject of prom didn't come up. After tonight, the answer is 'Yes.' The boy's got class!" Stockard said returning to her elation.

There was silence for a few minutes. Then Stockard said, "See you in the morning."

"Prom shopping, here we come!" Ashanti declared followed by, "See you in the morning."

## The Day After Yesterday

Stockard had planned to ride to school with her mom until Ashanti called and offered her a ride. Ms. Nicolette was all too eager for Stockard to accept the invitation. She had a busy morning; Ashanti's offer was a blessing.

When Ashanti pulled into the driveway and honked her horn, Stockard was still reminiscing over last night. She was processing the details that knocked her off her feet!

Stockard opened the passenger door of the silver sedan just as Ashanti was reaching for her bookbag to toss it into the rear passenger seat. "Still in heaven from last night?" Ashanti asked.

"Good morning to you, too," Stockard said maintaining her private thoughts.

"Good morning to you, too," Ashanti mocked. She loved her best friend, but there were days that her idiosyncrasies really got on her nerves. Today might just be one of those days. She could sense that something had triggered in her friend that was sending her to place that she did not seem to be in when she walked out of her front door. Stockard had a twilight in her eyes when she opened the car door; now the gaze was more distant.

"Did I tell you what we ate last night?" Ashanti asked trying to engage her friend. She was still in her ecstasy from last night and wanted her friend there, too.

"Did Fin's have Valentine's Day Special, too?" Stockard asked, adjusting herself in her seat.

"Yes," Ashanti answered. "We both had a Caesar salad. I had the garlic shrimp over angel hair with the lobster sauce. Javaris had the shrimp scampi with linguine."

"You look happy, Ashanti," Stockard said. "What was the atmosphere like?"

"The table had a floating candle. Everything was just perfect. Ladies were given a rose," Ashanti said trying to remember the fairy-tale experience while focusing on the traffic.

"Javaris looks so good, Stockard," Ashanti said. "I never realized how good he looks until last night."

"What did you wear?" Stockard asked.

"I borrowed my Aunt Dionne's red lace dress, the one she wore to Aunt Renee's 50th birthday party last year," Ashanti answered.

"You had to look good in that dress," Stockard said.

"I think Javaris liked what he saw," Ashanti said giving a flirty smile. She flicked her hair over her shoulder.

Ashanti looked at Stockard and said, "You wore the After-Christmas dress, right!"

"Yes, I wore the dress," Stockard answered.

"You probably knocked Chris off his feet," Ashanti said. "What did he wear?"

"He wore a pair of navy slacks with a wine-colored sweater. HE LOOKED GOOD!" Stockard admitted.

"Hold up! Wait a minute! Did I hear a twinkle in it?" Ashanti said.

"Whatever," was Stockard's response as she thought about how good Chris looked walking from her house to his car.

She secretly imagined what it would be like to be his prom date, his girlfriend. She had heard a rumor or two about him. Although she wasn't sure if all she heard was true or not, they played a major part in her decision to not give him an answer.

"You left out some details about night," Stockard said.

Ashanti parked her car. "After school," she replied.

Ashanti and Stockard joined the other students who were hurrying from the parking lot through the courtyard to their first period classes. Two additional police officers were on campus. Stockard and Ashanti had most classes in the same building. Having each other around made them feel more secure.

Stockard sat in her usual seat, readying herself for the pledge followed by the weather, news, and morning announcements.

"Good morning, Eastridge," Mr. Wilson's voice came across the intercom. "We at Eastridge are deeply sadden by the events that happened in Parkland, Florida on yesterday. The administration, faculty, and staff want you to know that we have taken every precaution to ensure nothing like that happens here at Eastridge. If you hear something or see something, please say something. The only way we can keep you safe is by being proactive. We have requested additional support to help us get through this time. Our district and community work very hard to keep all students safe. After we say the pledge, we will observe a moment of silence in remembrance of the event that happened in Parkland, Florida on yesterday. Have a good day."

Stockard was happy her first period was American History. Maybe Mr. Mason would allow them time to discuss the massacre.

"Do you seriously think we are safe at school, Mr. Mason?" a student in the last row asked.

"I believe we are safe here," Mr. Mason responded.

"Do we really need to have a fire drill every month?" another voice asked. So many school shootings happened after the sounding of the fire alarm, there was no wonder the student asked the question.

"The law requires schools to have some sort of drill at least once a month – tornado, earthquake, lockdown, or fire," the teacher responded.

"Did you have lockdown drills when you were in school?" Javaris asked. Stockard turned when she heard his voice and was surprised he was standing when he asked the question.

Javaris paced the floor when he was nervous, even if it meant within two steps on his desk. *He's nervous,* Stockard thought.

"No, Javaris, we did not have lockdown drills when I was in school. There were no threats of school shootings or intruders when I was in school," Mr. Mason answered.

"My mama said that people made bomb threats when she was in school. Did people make bomb threats at your school, too?" a girl in the second row asked.

"They did, but it was just a threat. No bomb was ever found in our school," Mr. Mason stated. "Typically, it was a kid who didn't want to go to school that day."

"That's the same thing my dad said," a voice from the center aisle said with relief.

"I don't think we have anything to worry about here," Mr. Mason said trying to calm his students.

"Yeah! That's what the teachers and students in Florida thought, too," the boy in the last row stated.

"Don't you think we need to do something about people having military style assault weapons?" the question came from the voice in the center aisle, the new student from California.

"It is people who kill people and not guns," Mr. Mason tried to reassure his students.

"I'm not saying that guns kill people. I am saying that military style assault weapons like the one used in Florida should not be in the hands of civilians," the boy from California said. "Who needs an AR-15, anyway?"

"People should be able to own whatever type of gun they want to own," chimed in another voice from the front row.

Mr. Mason decided to listen to the debate instead of interjecting his opinions or discussing any laws and regulations that govern fire arms.

"What do people need with a military style weapon? People cannot hunt with them. They destroy the animal. You can't eat them. Why kill an animal if you're not going to eat it?" argued the boy from California.

"What are you, some hippie or something?" asked the boy in the front row.

"No. I am just concerned that people are able to purchase weapons that were designed for the military," the boy from California said. "Do you know what they do to people?"

Stockard noticed that her classmates seemed to have lost interest in the debate. Sideline conversations began throughout the class.

Mr. Mason allowed his students to openly discuss their feelings. He knew they were trying to understand the events from yesterday. He understood their mental space; he, too, was trying to make sense of what had happened in Florida.

He allowed the discussions to continue for another five minutes before he said, "Take two laps then come back."

Mr. Mason gave them a lap or two around the corridor when they needed a break. Ninety minutes was a long time to sit in one class without the opportunity to move.

The Gilded Age was a subject that Stockard really enjoyed. She loved learning about industrial entrepreneurs and how their ingenuity catapulted America to become an international powerhouse. She was also inspired by the oil pipeline; she equated what the oil pipeline did for America to what the world wide web had done for a global society.

Stockard took her time shutting down her computer; her mind returned to last night's date. How could a day bring the same amount of joy as it brought pain?

It didn't matter that school massacres happened in other states. The violence impacted everyone everywhere. She was greeted by a smiling face as she reached the hallway.

"Are you always the last person to leave class?" Chris asked.

Was that an automatic smile she felt coming across her face? Stockard bit her upper lip in hopes of hiding the grin that she was unable to control. "No," she replied as she looked up at Chris with her huge, alluring eyes.

"I came to walk across the courtyard with you," he stated.

"Sure. I hope you won't be tardy," Stockard said.

"I'm in Building 1; you go to Building 2 for chemistry. I'm good," Chris said.

"And how do you know that?" Stockard asked forgetting to bite her lip to conceal the smile she was struggling to control.

"Javaris told me," Chris confessed.

"We do have first and second periods together," Stockard confirmed.

They walked across the courtyard to Building 2. Seven minutes was the amount of time Chris had to spend with Stockard and get to his next class. Those same seven minutes were the reasons why teachers did not want to allow students to go to the restroom during class. Teachers felt students had enough time to use the restroom and get to class if they used their time wisely. What they seemed to forget was that students needed time to socialize since they weren't allowed to use their phones during class.

The school district had blocked most social media sites since the big fight in October. Social media posts about the fight at Eastridge had sparked fights in the two other high schools in town. Social media was also blamed for the fights that were supposedly planned by two groups of girls. Word had gotten around to Eastridge administration before the plans were carried out. School Resource Officers from the neighboring middle and technology schools were called in as backup on Eastridge campus. The damage was minimal.

"Do you need a ride home after school?" Chris asked before leaving to walk to his class.

"I planned to go home with Ashanti," Stockard said. Dinner had transformed her feeling; but, no title changes yet.

"Okay. Just let me know if you need a ride," Chris said.

Chemistry was just chemistry. No one asked questions of the *Teacher of the Year*. They felt that chemistry teachers were more like scientists; they weren't really interested in government and politics.

Students settled in to continue to work on identifying compounds. They worked individually for about thirty minutes, then they worked in groups of three until it was time to compare answers with another group.

"Are you going home with Christ today?" Javaris asked.

"Whaat; what?" Stockard said looking up.

"Are you letting Chris take you home today?"

"I haven't even thought about that," Stockard responded.

"After last night, do I need to remind you of how much he likes you?" Javaris questioned, pleading his friend's case.

"Oh. Okay," Stockard said. She was caught off guard by his comment.

Javaris was usually trying to copy answers at the last minute since he spent so much time socializing during class.

Stockard really didn't want to talk about her relationship with Chris around other people. She wanted to make things official; but then again, she was scared.

"He said he wants ask you to the prom. I asked Ashanti," Javaris said.

"I know, 'Mr. Trey Songz'," Stockard said, trying to alert Javaris that she had been told about his Valentine's night.

"Let's get to work," she ordered.

"We can just copy your paper like we do most of the time," Javaris said.

"Not today," she said turning in her seat to work alone.

Javaris tapped Stockard's forearm. "Come on now; you don't need to act like that. I'll stop talking."

Stockard's no-nonsense work ethic was the reason why Javaris liked being in her group. He made better grades when he worked with Stockard. He was glad their groups paired up today. As the bell rang, he added, "If my man asks to drive you home, go with him."

"He already has," Stockard whispered to him. She flashed a smile with a twinkle in her eyes.

Javaris said, "That's what's up," giving Stockard a fist bump. Then he bopped out of the classroom in his usual swag to join the crowd in the hall.

Again, Stockard was among the last to leave the class. She really didn't like being in the ocean of people. She preferred as few people as possible. She walked towards the courtyard and saw Chris standing alone by a pillar.

"Can I walk with you to the café?" he asked.

"Sure," she said remembering to bite her upper lip to help conceal her feelings. They walked towards the café. Both were taken aback when they saw the television screens. "Is that Saved by the Bell?" Stockard asked.

The televisions were on the throwback sitcom, which was a welcome relief from the news shows they watched most days. Another television was showing an episode of A Different World. Stockard thought that no one paid attention to the televisions since there was no sound. Apparently, students did. Most people were looking at the screens.

Ashanti walked into the café with the posse' from gym class. Although she was putting on a happy face, Stockard read the stress lines in her face. Ashanti was going to Stepping Stones on a weekly basis and taking medication for depression. It was something about her eyes that were different than when they left the parking lot this morning.

Ashanti walked over to Stockard and whispered in her ear, "Javaris says that Chris wants to give you a ride home today."

"I don't' want to send the wrong message," Stockard said.

"He likes you. Let him give you a ride home," Ashanti said trying to encourage her friend.

"I will think about it next period," Stockard replied.

"Have your answer ready when he asks," Ashanti said.

"He's already asked," Stockard informed. "What about you?"

"I'm okay if you go," Ashanti reassured her.

Stockard was still trying to process her feelings for Chris. She had not done a lot of dating or even spent a lot of time talking to boys on a relationship level.

Most of Stockard's interactions with guys had been in class. She wasn't even sure if she would know what to do in a relationship. Some relationship things were off limits. How would a guy feel about that?

The last two classes seemed to go by with a breeze. Stockard decided to text Ashanti and let her know that if Chris was in the courtyard after school, she would ride home with him. Otherwise, she would ride home with her.

Chris was standing in the courtyard in her path to the parking lot. She was not sure if he was usually there since she was always focused on getting to cheerleading practice, her cello lessons, symphony, or home.

Chris drove the long way to Stockard house trying to spend as much time with her as possible.

"What time do you have to report to track practice?" she asked him.

"Coach wants us there and ready to run by 4:15. I'm good today. I have protein bars and water in my backpack," Chris answered. He thought about repeating his playlist. He decided to reserve that list for their date nights.

Stockard went to the kitchen to make a cucumber and mango smoothie before changing her clothes for the Y. She was determined to lose more weight before shopping for her prom dress. Three more weeks before her shopping trip was all the time she had left.

# The Movement Begins

It was official. Stockard was going to the prom with Chris. And she agreed to be his girlfriend.

Chris's promposal had come at the end of symphony two weeks after their Valentine's date. Garrison, one of the violinists from orchestra, started playing "Say Something Loving" through his blue tooth.

Everyone was startled. Chris opened the doors from the right aisle carrying a poster that read, "Stockard, say something loving. Please say "YES" to prom." Astonishment! Walking fifteen feet behind him were Michael, Javaris, and Ashanti.

The promposal was a little early, but Chris felt like he needed to do what a player had to do to get what he wanted.

\*\*\*\*\*\*\*\*\*\*\*\*\*\*\*\*\*\*\*\*\*\*\*\*\*\*\*\*\*\*\*\*\*\*\*\*\*\*\*\*\*\*\*\*\*\*\*\*

"He cheats on his girlfriends," girls would say.

"He hits his girlfriends," others would claim.

"He has an explosive temper," was the other innuendo.

Stockard had never seen that side of Chris. She did not know the person people were describing. Her decision to become his girlfriend was based on her experiences with him.

To make matters worse, Stockard encountered Brenna, Rian, and their group of friends sitting outside the café. Ashanti wasn't there.

"Look at her," she heard one voice say. "She thinks she got something, but he gonna' treat her like he did Shayla."

"How long do you think it will take him?" chimed in another voice.

"No time; he's already cheatin' on her," said the first voice.

"You say that like you know," said the second voice.

"BET! I know him! BET!" said the first voice.

*If he's cheating, I haven't loss anything,* Stockard thought. She was aware of how quickly relationships moved in high school. She was following Raven's advice from New Year's Eve night; her goodies were still in the jar.

The next morning in chemistry class, Stockard shared with Javaris her experience from lunch and the things people were saying in the hallways. It was no different than what she had heard once or twice in the past. Now it seemed more frequently. Comments seemed to be intentionally directed for her to hear. She began wondering if she made the right decision.

"People don't know what they're talking about," Javaris said. "Stick with what you know about him."

Very little changed in Stockard and Chris's relationship after it became official. He carried her home after school. They went on a date every Friday or Saturday night depending on Chris's work schedule. Intimacy was limited to second base. Stockard was dating Chris and had no intentions of marrying him or anyone else in the near future.

Stockard decided to take the relationship slow, real s-l-o-w. The slower she took the relationship, the less she had to deal with when it came to an end. Although her body told her she wanted something different, her mind cautioned her.

*********************************************

March 14, 2018 was *National School Walk-Out Day* to commemorate the students and faculty who lost their lives in Parkland, Florida on Bloody Wednesday. At 10:00 am, all students, teachers, and staff in schools across America would walk-out in protest of the gun violence that continued to plague the mental health of students and school personnel. Many students were ready to join a movement they felt empowered them to voice their pain.

Mr. Wilson and the Eastridge administrative team decided a more controlled protest would best fit their school. Their protest would be a walk-out into hallways to honor those who lost their lives by calling their names. Pictures of each victim would line the hallways and pillars of the school.

Stockard and Javaris stood beside each other. "I think we should've been able to walk down Main Street and not just stand in the hallway. What do they think we're going to do?" Stockard whispered to Javaris.

"It's just to keep us from getting too wilded up, I guess," he answered.

"Nobody is even talking about the march that is planned for the 24th," Stockard said.

"What march?" Javaris asked

"The *March for Our Lives* march," Stockard informed him.

"When did you hear about that?" Javaris probed.

"Okay, so Stacey and Raven were supposed to come carry us prom dress shopping Saturday morning, right? Well, they decided to postpone it until next weekend, so we could go to Winthrop to participate in the march. That's how I found out about it," Stockard told him.

"Who's going?" Javaris asked.

"My mom, of course. Michael, Ashanti, Stacey, Raven, and I think Raven is bringing Jade," Stockard said.

"What time is it?" Javaris continued to question.

"We are going to the campus at 9:30. The march begins at 10:00," Stockard said giving the details she had.

The hallways grew silent when Mr. Wilson began his announcement. The silence that stilled hallways was in remembrance of those who lost their lives. Silence triggered students to contemplate their own mortality; school was not as safe as it portrayed itself to be.

They were being reassured by their parents, friends, and school personnel that they were safe at Eastridge. The reassurance seemed to be for the person speaking the words.

Each of the seventeen names were called followed by 17 seconds of silence between each name. It was the silence between the names being called that created the most stress and anxiety in students and teachers. Was there ever a time in students' lives when lockdown drills were not a part of their emergency protocols? Was there ever a year when someone did not shoot in or at a school? How many teachers could recall a time when they were not threatened with school violence? For some it was bomb threats, for others it was school shootings.

*********************************************************

Second period class began a little late. Everyone was getting their minds adjusted to academics by 10:30. The one thing Stockard enjoyed about Mrs. White's class was the fact she made learning fun and enjoyable. She would adjust her lesson plans at the drop of a hat while still meeting her objective.

Mrs. White announced after the bell that declared students tardy, "I've decided to get our class started with a bit of yoga this morning. We will be following along with the instructor in the video. Is everyone ready?"

The routine began with students standing beside their desks, feet shoulder length apart. Eyes were closed. Deep breathing began. Heads were tilted back, eyes opened, and arms stretched to the ceiling. Arms were brought down parallel to students' shoulders for the first warrior pose. The second and third warrior poses followed. Stork poses, high lounges, revolving chairs, lord of the dance, downward dog, back to warrior 3, 2, and 1. Deep breathing before returning to their seats.

"The lord of the dance and downward dog are my favorite positions," a male voice from the back of the classroom said breaking the silence.

"Those are excellent stretches to get you focused, James," Mrs. White reminded him.

"I'd like to be the lord of your dance someday," the same voice whispered to a girl two rows over.

"If you had it, would you know what to do with it?" the girl answered back.

"Ancient Indians didn't write the Kama Sutra for us to not know anything," he whispered back.

"Karma what?" the girl asked.

"Kama Sutra. Yoga was invented for that," the boy said.

"Karma will get you," the girl replied, feeling insulted.

"I didn't say, 'karma;' I said, 'Kama Sutra,'" he said.

"Karma whatever back at you," she said.

Javaris whispered over to Stockard. "What is a Kama Sutra?"

"It's an ancient Indian text. He must be in the World Literature class. I heard they have been studying Vedic texts in Mr. Ashton's class. Ancient Indian writings are referred to as sutras or Vedas," Stockard instructed her friend. History was her thing.

"Is there anything you don't know?" Javaris asked.

"Yes; lots of things," Stockard answered.

\*\*\*\*\*\*\*\*\*\*\*\*\*\*\*\*\*\*\*\*\*\*\*\*\*\*\*\*\*\*\*\*\*\*\*\*\*\*\*\*\*\*\*\*\*\*\*\*\*\*\*\*

Stockard was a bit upset when Michael told her that they marched from their classrooms to the football. Michael, too, was upset about their march. He felt like they should have been allowed to march up or down the street.

Stockard reminded him that there were no sidewalks far enough to accommodate students leaving his campus. "We have sidewalks on both sides of our street, and we didn't leave campus. You only have walking trails."

News stations reported that some students were threatened with suspensions or expulsions if they participated in the walk-out. Some of the students who were threatened discussed how they felt their First Amendment rights had been violated, and how the Second Amendment rights were threatening their world. They were determined to have their concerns heard.

\*\*\*\*\*\*\*\*\*\*\*\*\*\*\*\*\*\*\*\*\*\*\*\*\*\*\*\*\*\*\*\*\*\*\*\*\*\*\*\*\*\*\*\*\*\*\*

Saturday morning, March 24, 7:30 am was the time alarms sounded in the Nicolette home. Breakfast had to be made, anxieties calmed, and expectations addressed before leaving. News shows were reporting on the highly anticipated event. 8:45 am, the doorbell rang. Javaris and Chris entered the home and were served what was left from breakfast.

"How many people do you think will be there today?" Michael asked.

"It's really hard to say. Some who plan to protest will march while others plan to attend the rally then leave. All of this has happened in such a short amount of time. Many groups many not be well organized," his mother answered. "Today is a history making day. Today you march for *your* life."

"Social media is not like regular media, Auntie," Stacey said. "Students around the world have organized marches on college campuses. Things have moved quickly."

"Around the world?" her aunt asked.

"Yes, around the world," Stacey confirmed.

\*\*\*\*\*\*\*\*\*\*\*\*\*\*\*\*\*\*\*\*\*\*\*\*\*\*\*\*\*\*\*\*\*\*\*\*\*\*\*\*\*\*\*\*\*\*\*

Protestors gathered with signs that read,

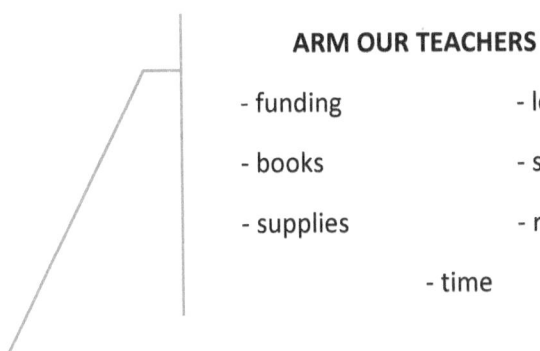

ARM OUR TEACHERS WITH

- funding          - less testing

- books            - support

- supplies         - resources

- time

**Today I turned 18**

**I will be voting**

**In 2018 and 2020**

Call Your State

Legislator!

People from all age groups and walks of life were ready to participate in the march. Several people talked about being a part of other marches throughout their lives.

Michael overheard one protestor say, "We've been told to watch out for counter- protestors. They are supposed to show up to bring a distraction to the march."

"Stockard, did you hear what they just said?" Michael inquired of his sister. He and Jade stood close to his mother. Since this was a new experience for the children, the mother wanted to keep them protected.

"I think we will be okay," Stockard said. She was not sure of her own words. She spoke them to comfort her brother. Chris took two steps closer to his girlfriend.

Stockard took deep breathes to calm herself. Not knowing what to expect was causing a panic attack. Her palms began to sweat; she rubbed them through her hair. She took a deep breath and swayed in place.

"Calm down," Chris said. "I got you."

"It's all the stuff she's seen in the movies and on television," Ashanti informed Chris and Javaris. "Did go you see *Selma*?" Ashanti asked the guys.

"No but I heard about it," Chris said.

"I didn't go either," Javaris said.

Stacey and Raven talked with a few of the organizers of the march then returned to their group. "A few people are going to make speeches. Then they will play "Shine" before we march to the Congressman's office downtown," Raven informed the group.

After the student body president and a few other students read their speeches, others joined in. One protestor was a retired teacher who had been injured in a school shooting over twenty-five years ago. He spoke about having PTSD because of the incident. Another protestor told the story of her mentee calling her during a lockdown drill and to say, "I love you." She said the little girl was afraid to go to school. A mother said her daughter refused to wear her favorite shoes to school again; her daughter thought the lights would give her location away to an intruder.

The march from Winthrop University to the US Representative's office was about a mile long. People shared stories of participating in marches during the Vietnam War, Civil Rights Movement, and for the annual Women's Rights marches of present day. The young adults listened to the memories that were shared among older friends that helped shaped their country. Progress had been made.

When they reached the congressman's office, protestors continued to speak. One lady told the story of being traumatized by the Columbine shooting. She described living through the post-traumatic event that forever changed her brother's life. "He suffers from mental health challenges. He struggles with employment. PTSD has become of part of his personality," she said.

Another student talked about losing her sister to a school shooting. She said that her life was never the same for several reasons. "My parents were afraid to send me to school, so I was homeschooled. Attending the university is a challenge. The sound of a bell is an anxiety trigger," the young woman said.

A teacher walked to the stage to plead his case and that of his colleagues, "Teachers need to have professionals in schools to help them deal with the mental health issues students are facing today. Guidance counselors can't do it by themselves."

As Stockard heard the teacher speak, something wailed up inside her that made her want to speak. At his conclusion, she walked to the front of the group and said that she felt like something needed to be done to help support students who believe laws should be changed with gun permits. She said, "Students should be allowed to exercise their first amendment rights without being threatened with punishment when something as serious as school shootings is being protested."

"Students are not against the 2$^{nd}$ Amendment; it is needed to protect citizens in another way. We are against permits being given to people who are a threat to themselves and others. Laws need to be changed to protect everyone," Stockard pleaded.

Javaris walked to the front with tears in his eyes. "Quin was my brother. He was shot in the park last summer. We became brothers when we fell out of a tree at my grandma's house. We shook our bloody hands and made a pact to be blood brothers. He was the only brother I ever had. I don't think people like Quin should lose their lives when they didn't do anything wrong," Javaris said, stating his case.

"Rise UP" was played after the last person spoke. Protestors left their posters and pictures of the victims from Parkland, Florida on the doorstep of the congressman's office.

"Members of congress decided to go on vacation," one protestor said. "Some even left the country."

\*\*\*\*\*\*\*\*\*\*\*\*\*\*\*\*\*\*\*\*\*\*\*\*\*\*\*\*\*\*\*\*\*\*\*\*\*\*\*\*\*\*\*\*\*\*\*

The group stopped by Kickstand for a bite to eat before they continued the next phase of their day. Televisions throughout the bar and grill were all tuned to the *March for Our Lives* event in the nation's capital. Students from Stoneman Douglas High School, siblings of shooting victims who lost their lives due to gun violence, and musical recording artists appeared on stage.

News reporters commented on the event with one reporter saying, "This new generation does not stick with anything. I wonder how long this movement will last?"

"As long as we want it to!" Ashanti responded to the reporter. She looked back at the television before the group disbursed to go shopping for prom dresses, work, and simply enjoy the weekend.

## Junior Prom

The Nicolette family liked to gather for important events. Once again, the crew gathered for a milestone that older cousins and other family members participate in. Stacey, Raven, and Jade assembled to do their masterpiece work on the bodies that had changed since Homecoming.

Michael joined his cousin Chauncey in doing a final detail check of the vehicle that would be used to transport the couples on their date. Chauncey owned the stretch limousine that would carry his cousin and her friends on their night out. This was his contribution to her prom. Careful detail was given to every feature on the vehicle to match the feelings both Michael and Chauncey had for Stockard.

"What do you think about your sister's date?" Chauncey questioned Michael.

"I like him. He's cool and all," Michael answered.

"Does he know how to treat a lady?" Chauncey asked.

"I guess you didn't hear about Valentine's."

"Tell me," Chauncey commanded.

Michael recounted the details he had overheard throughout the months. Chauncey nodded his head in approval.

"Where are they going tonight?" Chauncey asked.

"He's carrying her downtown to the City Club. They have a prom special," Michael informed his cousin.

"I can get with that," Chauncey said rubbing his beard.

Upstairs was busy with bubble baths, hair extensions, nail polish, and make-up. Music played in the background to get the girls in the mood for the night. At 4:18 on the dot, the young ladies emerged from upstairs. Chris and Javaris were waiting for the girls they worked so hard to attract as dates. Chauncey looked at his cousin and her friends before leaving them in the care of his driver.

Their first stop was the Fountain for a photo session. Chris and Javaris's parents were waiting when the limousine arrived. Tiffany and Lamont Simpson had been commissioned to apply their expertise for the session.

The Fountain was buzzing with other prom goers who were trying to accomplish the same goal. The couples were carefully situated to capture the rise and fall of the water.

Their next photo stop was Glencarin Gardens. The flowers in the garden complimented Stockard's light blue dress. The bodice had light and dark blue lace roses that were a perfect accent against the green leaves and pink tulips.

White gardenias and pink hydrangeas accented Ashanti's mint green dress. Her halter dress with sequin roses sparkled in the sunlight that was mostly hidden by magnolia trees.

The photo sessions wrapped up just in time to for the couples to make their dinner reservations. Water and crab cake appetizers were already placed on the table set for twelve people. The four other couples that sat at their table were from Rock Pointe and South Hill. Javaris and Chris knew three of the guys from football and track.

The salad course was next followed twenty minutes later was the opening of the buffet. Chicken Cordon Bleu, Prime Rib, and Chicken Marsala were entrée choices. Whipped potatoes, roasted potatoes, rice pilaf, garlic green beans, and broccoli were their choices for sides. Cheesecake closed out the dinner.

Back at Eastridge High School, red carpet greeted promgoers. Members from ENN worked hard to snap pictures and interview people as they made their way to the gym.

Mr. Wilson and members of his faculty and staff also greeted students. The music was loud, and the party was jumping when the couples stepped out the limo.

Stockard and Chris danced all night. Chris pulled his girlfriend close to him when he heard the opening chords of "Perfect" by Ed Sheeran. Stockard listened to the lyrics as Chris pulled back from her to look into her eyes. *Those eyes*, he thought, *make any guy want to take it to the next level.* He leaned down and give her a quick kiss.

Javaris looked at Ashanti then pulled her a little closer. "I've wanted to be my girl since the first day you came to our middle school," he whispered in her ear.

"Are you serious?" she asked looking into his eyes.

"Yeah. You're the perfect girl for me," he said.

The DJ played a mix of country, Hip Hop, Pop, and R&B music. Chris sang the lyrics to "Just the Way You Are" in Stockard's ear. She looked over and saw Javaris mouthing the words to the song, too.

Ashanti joined a few of her friends from gym class in the photobooth. Stockard joined friends from orchestra. Stockard had never felt more alive in her life. She was happy that she had Chris to help her enjoy the night. Ashanti was becoming her usual self again. Prom night was truly amazing.

Lights came on at 11:35. The extension Raven and Stacey had put in Stockard's hair was drenched with sweat. Ashanti's bangs were sticking to her forehead.

Chris and Javaris had loosened their bowties and unbuttoned the top three buttons on their shirts. Chris looked for his car in the parking lot. It had not moved from where he left it when Chauncey and Michael picked them up.

Chris drove by The Lake to check out the afterparty. Ashanti felt uneasy. That was the first time she had been there since Homecoming.

Sensing Ashanti's uneasiness, Javaris said, "Hey, man. We can't stay. I want to be home when people start coming."

Some of Javaris's friends from JROTC were already at his party when the couples arrived. Thai was acting as host until Javaris got there. He had blue toothed his phone to the speakers that were blaring Drake's "God's Plan."

People were taking selfies and posting them on social media. They were checking their accounts to get the latest news on what was going on around town.

Several of Javaris's guests were from other schools in the area. A few people he didn't know were there, too. "As long as we don't have any drama, I'm cool with them staying," Javaris told Thai.

The party ended when the sun began to rise. Javaris looked around his backyard; clean up would be easy. His yard hadn't been trashed.

Chris, Ashanti, and Stockard began helping Javaris pick-up the garbage that was lying around. His parents came out to help.

"Go ahead and take the young ladies home. We'll finish this off," Javaris's dad ordered Chris.

Chris obeyed the command and carried the girls to the Nicolette home.

"See you later?" he asked Stockard giving her one final embrace and kiss to seal the occasion.

"I'll call you," she answered. Pulling an all-nighter was not something that Stockard typically did. As a matter of fact, this was the first time she had ever experienced one. The sleep was coming on.

"Did you have fun?" Michael asked as she and Ashanti walked to the stairs.

"What are you doing up so early? Have you been waiting for us all night?" Stockard asked.

"Waiting on you. I took naps," he said.

"Waiting on me?" She asked for clarity.

"Yeah, waiting on you and Ashanti," Michael confirmed.

"We had a great time," she said. "Thanks for waiting up and helping Chauncey with the car."

Michael was still trying to get used to the new Stockard. She was being nice to him. He was enjoying his new sister but missing the old one, too.

"I'm going to bed," he said. "Good night or morning. Whatever it's supposed to be."

"I'm right behind you," said Ashanti.

"Call your grandmother first," Michael said. "She wants to hear from you."

# The Weeks After Prom

Monday morning was exciting and a drag. Students who had pulled an all-weekender were feeling jetlagged but still participated in the post-prom joy. People were sharing their pictures from prom night with their peers and teachers.

Girls were in heaven. Guys who had captured their perfect date were still floating on Cloud 9. Eastridge High School was bustling with joy.

Stockard settled into getting ready for the Small & Solo Ensemble competition. She had spent her lesson and enrichment times practicing "The Swan" to perfect her technique.

"Oh, no!" She said one day during Enrichment. "My D-string popped."

Stockard immediately called her mother for help. "Mama, could you pleaseee call The Violin Shoppe to see if they can replace my strings today? I only have one week before my performance!"

"Do you not have symphony after school today?" her mother asked.

"I can't go to symphony with a broken "D" string!" Stockard exclaimed.

The Violin Shoppe was the place Ms. Nicolette relied on to keep Stockard's cello in tip-top shape. Stockard was the first person in her family to play a string instrument that wasn't a piano. Brass and woodwinds were the instruments people in her family played.

Stockard was trying her best to earn a "Superior" rating on her performance. She had worked hard on increasing her confidence and wrist movements. She was committed to music and was considering it as major in college.

Playing her cello was one the things that helped Stockard with her anxiety and depression. Music therapy had been proven to be an excellent way to improve mental health. All the therapies and coping strategies were working. She and her therapist had agreed to her attending therapy on an irregular basis. Stockard wanted to try managing her life without weekly or bi-weekly sessions.

\*\*\*\*\*\*\*\*\*\*\*\*\*\*\*\*\*\*\*\*\*\*\*\*\*\*\*\*\*\*\*\*\*\*\*\*\*\*\*\*\*\*\*\*\*\*\*\*

"Could you ride home with me today?" Read a text message from Ashanti.

Stockard replied, "Okay."

"I'm riding home with Ashanti today," Stockard texted Chris.

"Y?" he asked.

"Apparently she needs to talk. Just got the message." Followed by a smiley face with hearts in the eyes.

"Back to you," was his response.

\*\*\*\*\*\*\*\*\*\*\*\*\*\*\*\*\*\*\*\*\*\*\*\*\*\*\*\*\*\*\*\*\*\*\*\*\*\*\*\*\*\*\*\*\*\*\*\*

Stockard met Ashanti at her car. She slid into the passenger seat as usual. Stockard was having second thoughts about driving. Her anxiety had crippled her ability to drive. Stockard was beginning to feel that she could be more of a help to her friend if she did some of the driving.

"Do you know Chloe?" Ashanti asked.

"The girl in your government class?" Stockard inquired.

"Yeah, that one. Zoe told me that something happened to her at The Lake Saturday night," Ashanti said.

"Something like what?" Stockard questioned.

"Similar to what happened to me," Ashanti said.

"Does Zoe know what happened to you?"

"No, nobody knows except us. People were talking about it in the locker room. They said that she was down at the boat slip for hours before her friends missed her," Ashanti informed.

"Who did she go to the prom with?" Stockard inquired.

"She went with a group of friends. They said that she walked to the boat slip to get beer. Her friends couldn't find her when it was time to go. When they saw her at the boat slip, she was under the influence of something. She had a hard time coming to. She had some injuries and stuff like that."

"Oh My God!" Stockard cried, putting both hands over her mouth. "Did they get the person who did that to her?"

"Nobody knows who did it. Do you think there might be a serial rapist or something running around?" Ashanti asked.

Stockard wanted to ask her friend if she had been violated that night. Ashanti grew quiet, so Stockard decided not to ask.

"Do you think I should've reported what happened to me to the police?" Ashanti asked.

"What do you mean?" Stockard asked hoping for more details.

"I don't think I was fully raped, but I'm not sure. I know that I was sore down there, but my panties were still on. One thing that was strange is that... is that... is that..." Ashanti could not finish sharing her memory.

"Do you still see your therapist every week?" Stockard asked.

Ashanti nodded her head up and down to answer, "Yes."

"What does she say?" Stockard inquired.

"I haven't been able to open up to her about a lot of stuff. I think I intentionally block bad memories out of my mind. Sometimes the emotional pain is too much," Ashanti confessed.

"I know," Stockard said going into a memory of her own. "I'm always here for you," Stockard reassured her friend.

"Have you and Chris had sex yet?" Ashanti probed.

"No, not yet. I can tell he wants to, though."

"What do you want to do?" Ashanti asked.

"I'm not ready. What about you and Javaris?"

"I'm not ready, either. Sometimes I want to, but other times I not sure. I don't want to get pregnant or disappoint my grandma," Ashanti said. "I'm not even sure if I can."

Stockard responded, "I know. We have enough girls in our class who are pregnant. I feel the same way. I promised myself I wasn't going to have sex until college. I don't want any distractions that would keep me from my goals."

"How long do you think they will wait?" Ashanti asked.

"I don't know. But I'm not going to let that pressure me into doing something I don't want to do," Stockard said.

\*\*\*\*\*\*\*\*\*\*\*\*\*\*\*\*\*\*\*\*\*\*\*\*\*\*\*\*\*\*\*\*\*\*\*\*\*\*\*\*\*\*\*\*\*\*\*\*\*

On the morning of her solo performance, Chris gave his girlfriend a kiss for good luck. Stockard was shocked by her reaction to the kiss. Her body responded in a way she had never felt.

Stockard reached her goal; she had perfected "The Swan." She earned the "Superior" rating she was hoping for. She was pleased with herself and excited to share the news with the people she loved the most. First, she texted her boyfriend, then her mother and brother, finally Ashanti.

"CONGRATULATIONS! Ride home with me," was Ashanti's response.

"CONGRATULATIONS!!!!" was Chris's response with at thumbs up emoji.

"Riding home with Ashanti," Stockard replied to Chris.

"Y," he texted back.

"She must have something to talk about," Stockard wrote.

\*\*\*\*\*\*\*\*\*\*\*\*\*\*\*\*\*\*\*\*\*\*\*\*\*\*\*\*\*\*\*\*\*\*\*\*\*\*\*\*\*\*\*\*\*\*

"It happened again!" Ashanti said to Stockard.

"What happened again?" Stockard was lost in her performance and love for Chris.

"The boat slip, The Lake," Ashanti stated.

"Do you mean to tell me," Stockard began.

"Yep, the same thing happened again. This time the girl went to the police," Ashanti explained.

"Who was it?" Stockard inquired.

"They're not saying who it is. Tina's dad told her to stay away from the boat slip at The Lake because a girl was raped there Friday night," Ashanti said extending the warning.

"So that's not the same person then," Stockard said.

"Nope," Ashanti said lowering her head.

"Do you think there is a serial rapist on the lose?"

"Three people WE know about; I think it's serial," Ashanti sadly replied.

"Who do you think it could be?" Stockard asked.

"I have no idea. I just know that I'm feeling a little guilty and wonder if I should say something," Ashanti asserted.

"Did you talk to your grandma and aunt about it?"

"You know that I can't talk to them about this sort of stuff," Ashanti said, shifting her eyes to the sky.

"You know if you talk to my mom she is going to tell your grandma," Stockard reminded her.

"I know," Ashanti said not removing her gaze.

"What should we do?" Stockard asked.

"My therapist said that it's my choice. Hopefully, now that someone has come forward about what has happened to her, they will catch him," Ashanti wished out loud.

Two more girls came forward with similar stories. Either they were able to escape the attacker, or the attack was successful.

Ashanti didn't want to bring attention to herself, so she decided to remain silent. She wondered how many other girls made the same decision. With the number of reports that had been made, she felt confident the attacker would soon be caught.

*********************************************

"Javaris, what was Chris like when he dated other girls," Stockard asked shocking him with the question before first period.

"Where did this come from?" he asked.

"It seems like people are talking more and more about him having a temper, hitting girls, and cheating."

Javaris tried to make her feel secure in her relationship by saying, "First of all, I know you and Chris haven't gone all the way. He respects you too much for that. He really likes you. He's not the kind of guy to hit girls unless he has to defend himself."

"What about his temper?" she probed.

"Who doesn't have a temper? He's a football player. His temper is like everybody else's," Javaris said defending Chris.

As soon as Javaris had the opportunity, he typed in his phone, "I need to talk to you." Just as he hit 'send' a thought crossed his mind. *My dad hates when my mom says, "We need to talk." That meant something serious was going on.* He hoped Chris didn't get alarmed.

**************************************************

"What's up?" Chris asked Javaris in the parking lot after school. They were both happy that Ashanti asked Stockard to ride home with her again. This was becoming a habit.

"Are you still hittin' ole' girl?" Javaris asked.

"What you are talkin' about?" Chris questioned.

"Who you hittin', man? People are saying things in the hall so that Stockard can hear it. You know its Brenna and Rian. They had her all upset a few weeks ago. Who you hittin'? I know Stockard hasn't given it up yet; Ashanti told me," Javaris said.

"I kick it with Brenna every now and again. That's something been going on since I caught Shayla with that dude. She kno' ain't nothin' between me and her," Chris confessed to his friend.

"Hey, man. You might wanna stop that. That's why she's so mad at Stockard. How does she feel about you?" Javaris asked.

"What you mean by that? I used to date her best friend, man. She knows the rules," Chris answered.

"She broke the rules. You broke the rules," Javaris reminded him. Silence remained between them.

"I don't know what you're gonna do about this one. Brenna must want more from you," Javaris warned his friend.

"Stop when Stockard gives it up," Chris said. "I'm not a cheater, but I have needs."

"It won't be that easy, man. I'm tellin' you. Ole' girl trippin'. You better watch out for that, Chris," Javaris said.

"Look. Stockard is the girl I've wanted to date since ninth grade. I never thought I had a chance with her because she's so smart and beautiful. Brenna calls me. I give her what she wants. I don't see it as cheatin'," Chris rationalized.

"Neither one of them might not see it that way. You know how girls get in their feelin's and stuff," Javaris reminded him.

"I got you," Chris said. "Thanks for the info."

*****************************************************

The second of the big three tests given to juniors had finally been administered. The "Ready for Work and College Assessment" was much easier than they thought. "It was common sense," remarked most students.

The final test for juniors was the American Government/History exam. The results from that test counted twenty percent of their final grade. *It would have been nice for the test to had been broken up into semesters,* many students thought.

Juniors were also required to do a United State history or government presentation. Stockard wanted to do her project on music during the 1960's. She ended up with the Roaring 20's. She helped Chris with his presentation on the Harlem Renaissance.

"It would be nice if our teachers accepted a project on art in the 1920's," Stockard said. "It would make things a lot easier for both of us," she told Chris.

Although Chris worked hard on his studies, the history project was not something he could focus on. He planned to major in finance. Some day he would become a business man, an entrepreneur even like his dad. He accepted two invitations to visit D-1 schools during his Spring Break. He paid close attention to the things they said about majors. Finance was not something most athletes majored in. That did not deter Chris from his decision. The only way he could do it was to put more effort into his studies.

He knew he would achieve his goals. Setting and achieving goals had become second nature. One major goal he had set for himself at the beginning of the school year had already been accomplished. He was dating the girl that his teammates said you don't date in high school. They were right about one thing — girls like that are not easy. That didn't matter to him as much as having her on his arm. Nobody knew what happened between them when they were alone. Besides, when they did go all the way, it was would be nice to know he was her first.

## The Summer After Junior

Ever since he became principal of Eastridge High School, Mr. Wilson announced the beginning of summer break with "Summertime" by DJ Jazzy Jeff and the Fresh Prince. The summer of 2018 was no different.

Stockard, Ashanti, Chris, and Javaris were feeling confident about going into their last summer as "kids". Everyone knew they had earned every credit attempted during their second semester. The only thing that concerned them was whether they were maintaining the grade point average and class rank they were hoping to enter their senior year with.

Stockard and Ashanti would be touring several colleges across Georgia and the Carolinas during a college tour week. Chris would alternate his time between football camps and college tours. Since Javaris was having second thoughts about college, he decided to tour a few colleges, too. He had promised his dad that he would either do Air Force Reserves or Active Duty. He wanted to keep his options open.

Another tradition for juniors at Eastridge High School was to attend the amusement park the first Friday after school ended. Everyone looked forward to riding the Terminator and Fury 365, some of the best rollercoasters in the country, and the waterpark that seemed to get better every year.

Chris, being the star cornerback, attended several graduation parties the following night. Eastridge and the other high schools in town always graduated on Saturday. Chris attended parties hosted by people from the other high schools, too. Once football season was over, the competition was over, which meant all was well among friends again.

Summertime was also the time when people have backyard bar-b-ques and yard parties every weekend. Ms. Nicolette was busy planning her annual Low Country Boil for her family, which kicked off the July 4th celebrations. Family would be arriving in town in just a couple weeks, so she had to make sure every detail was covered with Slow Smokin' Bar-B-Que.

"WHAT!" the sound from upstairs interrupted Ms. Nicolette thoughts. She called upstairs to the noise to see what was going on. Michael and Stockard ran into the kitchen.

"NO! This can't be true!" Michael said shaking his head while looking at this phone.

"Let me check!" Stockard said.

"Check what?" their mother asked.

"THIS!" Michael said handing his mother his cell phone. Shaking his head, he said, "This can't be true. This can't be true. People need to stop playing, bruh!"

Stockard checked her social media accounts. She saw posts that all said the same thing. She called Stacey;

apparently her phone was off because it went straight to voice mail. She called Raven; straight to voice mail. She called Ashanti, "Are you still at work?"

"Yeah, and it's bad, gurl! People are pretty much going crazy around here! I can't talk right now. I'll have to call you back!" Ashanti said panicking.

Michael looked at Stockard, "Is it true? Is it true, Stockard?" He questioned his sister with tears in his eyes.

"It can't be true," he said shaking his head, voice was trailing off into a whisper.

Stockard looked at her brother trying to fight back her own tears. She looked at her mother trying to get some help, but there was nothing she could be done to help with this moment.

"I believe it is true, Michael," Stockard answered still trying to fight back the tears that were about to become rip-roarin'-rapids. "I'm so sorry," she said to her brother before embracing him. "I'm so sorry," she said again.

This was one moment Stockard wished she could take back. This was one moment she had never prepared for.

Some of her tears were for the pain she knew her brother felt; the others were for Raven; the remaining were for the pain she felt.

A light had gone out in the universe that would never again shine its radiance in this world, in this place, in this space, in this time.

Never again would she see the dance moves, have the finishing touches on her make-up, or the company that brought so much life to a party.

Everyone paused when she walked into the room; it was just something about her that made people take notice. Was it her confidence? Was it her smile? Was it her beauty, or was it her style? Stockard had always heard of the "IT Factor;" the thing that cannot be described by words, but you know IT when you see IT.

Jade had the "IT Factor!" She could do anything she put her mind to. Everyone on social media loved to see her live dancing videos. They looked forward to the latest make-up styles she would create to give them inspiration on how to be on fleek. Girls wanted to be her, and every boy wanted to date her, including Michael.

It was during *First Night* that Michael fell in love with her. He would ask Stacey to bring her over whenever he knew she and Raven would be around. Jade would play basketball with him, which was another reason he loved her so much.

Stockard had never seen her brother cry like that. She felt powerless in the moment. She had always been able to say or do something to make him feel better. But not that tonight. Nothing in her life had prepared her for that moment.

Her thoughts were interrupted by the doorbell. She looked over at Michael, who had his head in their mother's lap. She walked slowly to the door to see who was there. She opened it.

"I had to come check on my little homey," Chris said. He briefly hugged Stockard before making his way to the family room. He didn't know what he would say to Michael when he got here. He just knew that he wanted to make sure he would be okay. Chris wanted to make sure that he would be okay, too. Once again, he was questioning his own mortality.

Michael sat up from his mother's lap when he saw Chris. He tried to pull himself together. He could only muster up enough strength to sit-up.

Chris walked over to where Michael sat and put his arm around his shoulder, a move his father made when he was having a hard time. Chris could tell that the typical bro' hug would take too energy.

"Hey, Man. It's gonna be all right," Chris said. He really didn't know what else to say to him. He tried to think of what his dad had said to him last summer when Quin died. He couldn't remember. The night brought back so many memories of last summer.

"Turn on the TV," Michael said. "I wanna see what the news shows have to say."

Ms. Nicolette didn't want to honor the request. She thought it might be too upsetting for him. She obliged her son. She did not know what he would need to get him through the nights and days ahead. The doorbell rang again, and this time, Ms. Nicolette answered. Javaris and Ashanti joined the group.

"Breaking News!" came across the television screen. Everyone in the room braced themselves for the news flash. The news reported:

"A man who appeared to be in his 20's came racing through a yard where a family bar-b-que was being held. Moments later, shots were fired at the young man who continued to run. A 14-year-old female who was attending the event was accidently hit by one of the bullets. She was taken to the local emergency room with an excessive amount of blood loss. She has been pronounced..."

Ms. Nicolette turned the channel. The final words did not need to be heard. Enough had been said! She looked at the children sitting in the room. It could have been her home and the event she was planning. Feeling frustrated and dejected, she left the room, so the children could grieve. She needed to grieve the way a mother would grieve.

The room was silent. Ashanti and Chris checked their phones for social media posts. Pictures of Jade flooded their feeds. Friends were posting and reposting their favorite memories.

The media covered the news the entire week. Social media account holders continued to be post and repost their fondest memories. Parents posted on social media about how their children were trying to cope with the loss of their friend. Jade was so young and well loved.

A candlelight vigil was held at the fountain for the soul that illuminated the lives of family, friends, and teachers. People from around the area joined the vigil in support of the young lady that brought joy to so many lives.

Stockard looked at the flames that were flickering in the night. Then she casted her gaze to the stars shining so bright. *We have to do something because we can't forget*, she thought to herself. *Jade's life has got to mean something forever. Quin's life must give us all meaning, and so does Crystal's life.*

Crystal was the young lady whose life was cut short due to mental health complications. Stockard kept that life in her heart. She identified with some of the health challenges. Crystal was not talked about among the kids. Could it be that Crystal's challenges reminded them of their own struggles? She was someone Stockard vowed to never forget.

The Low Country Boil was something many family members looked forward to. Stacey and Raven were there to help as usual. Stockard shared an idea she had discussed with her friends and with Raven and Stockard. They agreed that her idea was a good way to address the issues she had on her mind. She decided to run the idea by an older cousin, a sociology professor.

"Dr. Hughes," Stockard addressed her cousin. "I want to ask your opinion on something." She detailed the events that had impacted their community in the past year or so. She talked about how people in the media doubted that the *March for Our Lives* movement would sustain. She told him how she wanted to normalize something that she saw as a major issue when it comes to violence. He listened intentionally and agreed with her observations.

"What you think about the name — YAMHA?" she asked.

"How are you spelling that?" he asked.

"Y-A-M-H-A; it is an acronym for Young Adults Mental Health Alliance," she explained.

"Young Adult Mental Health Alliance," he pondered while shaking his head. "I like it."

\*\*\*\*\*\*\*\*\*\*\*\*\*\*\*\*\*\*\*\*\*\*\*\*\*\*\*\*\*\*\*\*\*\*\*\*\*\*\*\*\*\*\*\*\*\*\*\*\*\*\*\*

Raven and Stacey carried Stockard to the voter registration office.

"You know that registering on your 18th birthday is a family tradition. How are you going to explain this to Aunt Jeanie?" Stacey questioned.

Joyce C. Cooper

"The same way I explain everything else – with my mouth," Stockard replied.

Chris, who turned 18 in December, and Javaris, who would turn 18 in October, registered to vote, too. Ashanti wouldn't turn 18 until the following year, so she went along for the ride. Michael joined, too.

Stockard shared her news with her mother. She told her mother how she felt empowered to do something now that she had registered to vote.

"Stacey and Raven are going to help us organize a voter registration drive before school starts. We have decided to set-up a booth in the breezeway to catch students when they register for classes," Stockard said.

She looked at her baby brother. She remembered the day he was born. She looked at Raven. She thought about Jade and wanted her life to mean something. She also wanted to do something for Raven and her family to let them know that Jade's light continues to exist in the universe.

She asked her friends what they thought about purchasing the naming of a star for Jade.

"What are you talking about?" Javaris asked.

"I've never heard of that," Chris added.

"There you go with that universe stuff again," Michael chimed in.

*Where did he come from?* Stockard thought to herself.

"I like it," Ashanti said. "My aunt named a star for her poodle a couple years ago."

"That's exactly where I got that idea from," Stockard admitted.

"You mean to tell me that people actually do that stuff?" Javaris questioned.

Stockard used her phone to search for star-naming companies. Ashanti directed her to the website her aunt used.

"They give you a certificate with the coordinates of the star from Earth and everything," Ashanti added.

"I guess that would be a good thing to do," Chris said.

Javaris and Michael concurred.

A candlelight vigil was held the first week in September. Enough money had been donated to purchase three stars to be named – Crystal, Quin, and Jade. Students from around the city joined in to help celebrate the lives that were lost to mental health complications and gun violence. "Shine" was played and doves released as everyone stood in silence to remember those that were now watching over them for all eternity.

# Recommendations from the Author

Mental health is just as important as any other health issue. Schools are increasingly challenged with addressing mental health issues in students. Mindfulness and meditation have proven to be excellent tools to help students successfully manage anxiety and depression. For more information on anxiety and depression, please visit the Anxiety and Depression Association of America's website at https://adaa.org/understanding-anxiety/depression.

Mass school shootings have plagued the lives of American students and school personnel for decades. Some students and teachers display symptoms of post-traumatic stress disorder. For more information about PTSD, please use the following link provided by the United States Department of Veterans Affairs: https://www.ptsd.va.gov/public/ptsd-overview/basics/symptoms_of_ptsd.asp.

Misunderstandings surround the subject of consent when it comes to sexual encounters. If you need more information about rape or have been a victim and need help, please call The National Sexual Assault Hotline at 800.656.HOPE/800.656.4673 or visit the RAINN website at https://hotline.rainn.org/online/.

NAMI, National Alliance on Mental Illness, is a valuable resource to help you connect with mental health treatment in your area. Please visit their website at https://www.nami.org/.

September is Recovery Awareness Month. The Substance Abuse Mental Health Services Administration's theme for this year is "Join the Voices of Recovery: Invest in Home, Health, Purpose, and Community. Please visit their website if you need help or treatment. https://www.samhsa.gov/find-help.

.